Textrovert

Textrovert

Lindsey
Summers

wattpad

KCP Loft is an imprint of Kids Can Press

Kids Can Press gratefully acknowledges the financial support of the Government of Ontario, through the Ontario Media Development Corporation.

Published in Canada and the U.S. by Kids Can Press Ltd.
25 Dockside Drive, Toronto, ON M5A 0B5

Kids Can Press is a Corus Entertainment Inc. company

www.kidscanpress.com
www.kcploft.com

The text is set in Adobe Text Pro and Museo Sans

Edited by Kate Egan
Designed by Michel Vrana
Jacket photo courtesy of Stocksy

Printed and bound in Altona, Manitoba, Canada, in 10/2016 by Friesens Corp.

CM 17 0 9 8 7 6 5 4 3 2 1

Library and Archives Canada Cataloguing in Publication

Summers, Lindsey, author

Textrovert / written by Lindsey Summers.

ISBN 978-1-77138-735-4 (hardback)

I. Title.

PZ7.1.S94Te 2017   j813'.6   C2016-902743-0

FSC
www.fsc.org
MIX
Paper from
responsible sources
FSC® C016245

For my Wattpad readers, I love you guys

Chapter 1

iLost My Phone

• • •

Fate had a twisted sense of humor. Either that or it hated her, because there was no way she should have been paired with a twin like this.

"Come on, Keels," Zach pleaded. The wide-eyed, earnest expression might work on their mother, but Keeley knew better.

"You're not getting the keys," she told him.

"Please?"

"No way."

"You've had the car all day."

"And you got up an hour ago."

"So?" he taunted, acting nowhere near seventeen.

"It's already dark. That's a problem."

"It's summer. And you shouldn't be talking. You slept till noon yesterday."

She was hoping he'd missed that. "I was tired."

"Because reading is so exhausting."

"You don't get it." Marathon reading wasn't for the faint of heart. It took dedication and a big bladder to sit on a chair for hours on end.

Zach scoffed. "The only time you move is to turn a page or grab a snack."

"But I'm moving up here," she told him, tapping her temple.

"Keeley," he said in that placating tone that drove her nuts. "This is my first day off in three weeks, and as captain of the varsity football team —"

She rolled her brown eyes, the rich color identical to his. If she had to listen to his Mr. I-Am-Captain-Therefore-I-Am-God speech one more time, she'd pop him in the nose. He'd been strutting around the house ever since the team voted two weeks ago. Not that the decision was surprising. Zach was a natural leader. She just wished he would leave the need to control on the field. His attitude got real old, real fast.

"Mom and Dad gave the car to both of us so I have as much right to use it as you do," he concluded.

"And you drive it ninety percent of the time."

"Because I'm the one who actually *needs* it."

The implication hurt, but she let it go. It wasn't worth the headache. "Well, I need it now. The fair closes in thirty minutes."

"Then get Nicky to drive you home. I'm sure she's here somewhere."

Of course Nicky was here. They'd been best friends since kindergarten. Most people considered Nicky her twin, not Zach. But keeping the car was about principles. Keeley had the keys first, therefore she got the car, even if there was someone else to give her a ride.

Just then Nicky came back from scoping out the line at the Ferris wheel. "It's not too long," she said. "But the fair closes in twenty minutes, so we should head over." Every year the girls rode it as their last hurrah of summer. Zach used to come with, but he stopped once they started middle school. Claimed he was above something so juvenile.

"See? Now hand over the keys," Zach said, wiggling his fingers in Keeley's face. "I have things to do."

Keeley batted his hand away. "Why are you in such a rush?"

"Does it matter?"

That's when she knew. "You're going to Cort's house." Cort was Zach's best friend. He threw legendary parties whenever his parents were out of town. "I thought he was away for the weekend."

"He decided to stay home." Rubbing the back of his neck, Zach let out a long sigh. "Listen, if you give me the keys, I'll let you copy my homework."

It was a tempting offer since she hadn't opened a single textbook all summer. Enrolling in AP classes had seemed like a good idea last spring, especially because Zach and Nicky were in them, too, but now that summer was over and she was faced with a year of college-level work ... well, regret was creeping in.

"And I'll do your chores for a week," he added.

"A month," she countered.

"Two weeks."

"Three."

"Two and a half." When she started to protest, he tugged at the end of her ponytail, just like he used to when they were little. "Please? For me?"

She felt herself softening. Damn it. He didn't play fair. "Only if you promise to call if you need a ride home." Zach didn't drink a lot, but when he did, he went full throttle. She was always worried he might do something stupid like drink and drive. He was annoying, but he was her brother. She didn't want anything bad to happen to him. If she didn't look out for him, who would?

"And you'll cover for me with the parentals?" he asked.

She tossed him the keys. "Don't I always?"

"You're the best," he called over his shoulder as he jogged away.

"I think I know why he's in such a hurry," Nicky commented. She nodded toward a stunning redhead with fair skin and cleavage Keeley could only dream of. Zach leaned down to whisper in the girl's ear, then hooked an arm around her waist and led her to the exit.

"Not in the car. Absolutely not." Keeley dug in her purse, ready to call and chew him out. The last time Zach took a girl for a ride, Keeley found a bra in the backseat. "Um, Nicky ... you wouldn't happen to have my cell, would you?"

"Not again," Nicky groaned. "This is the third one you've lost in six months."

"You don't have to remind me. I was there," said Keeley. Her parents' lecture on responsibility still burned in her mind. "Do you have it?"

"You never gave it to me."

Cursing, Keeley sunk to her knees and dumped out her purse. She had to find that phone. Her parents would refuse to buy another one, and there was no way she was starting senior year cell-less.

Nicky crouched next to her. "You had it when we were pigging out on funnel cakes. I remember because Zach kept texting you."

"Right." Keeley had swallowed the last bite of funnel cake, downed the rest of her vanilla shake, grabbed her purse and then — "Crap! I think I left it on the table." Her parents were going to kill her. That phone was brand new. She hadn't even bought a case for it yet or downloaded any apps.

Nicky helped scoop up her stuff. "It's only been half an hour. It could still be there."

Biting her lip, Keeley glanced at the Ferris wheel. There was no way they could dash across the fairground to the food area and still make it back in time. But they couldn't *not* ride. It was tradition. Pushing herself off the ground, Keeley slung her purse over her shoulder and took off running. "Get in line," she yelled, ignoring Nicky's confused yelp. "I'll meet you there!"

Weaving her way through the crowds, she moved as quickly as she could, but there were too many people. Seeing a clear path around the perimeter of the fairground, she dashed to the outside edge and sprinted the rest of the way to the food area. Gasping for air, Keeley spotted the table and slowed to a walk, both legs trembling.

"Fifteen minutes. Fifteen minutes till the fair closes," a voice announced over the loudspeaker.

"Please, please, please," she chanted. But when she got to the table, it was empty. Frustrated, Keeley kicked a chair and it toppled over. People started staring, some even pulling out their phones to record her. Face red, Keeley bent down to right it. That's when she spotted a black phone lying underneath the table, hidden by a patch of weeds. *Yes!* Luck was totally on her side today.

By the time she reached the Ferris wheel, Nicky was almost at the front of the line. "Did you find it?" Nicky asked as Keeley squeezed her way through.

Grinning, Keeley gave a thumbs-up. Nicky shook her head like she couldn't believe Keeley's luck. And frankly, neither could Keeley. It was a good thing she found it, too. She hadn't programmed a password yet. Zach had told her to as soon as she got it, but she'd ignored him. Maybe she would keep this incident to herself. Didn't want to hear the "I told you so." She hated that phrase. Was already bracing herself because she knew she'd hear it when he handed her his summer homework. *But maybe* ... Keeley eyed Nicky. "*Soo* ... how's the homework coming? You finished yet?"

A knowing smirk. "I thought you were copying off Zach."

"I can't copy word for word. The teachers will notice."

"What do you have left?" asked Nicky.

Keeley's expression turned sheepish. "All of it." She'd been *meaning* to start all summer.

"Why am I not surprised?"

"Procrastination invigorates me," Keeley insisted.

"And leaves you panicking. If you start tonight, you should finish in time. We have almost two weeks left." Nicky never left anything last minute. She was almost as prepared as Zach.

The line moved forward, and soon they were ushered to the loading area. One by one, the cars stopped at the bottom and people were let off and on. When it was their turn, Keeley carefully stepped into the swaying carriage and settled next to Nicky. They jerked forward as the ride started spinning.

"Then what about going to the library with me tomorrow?" Keeley asked her. Maybe she could convince Nicky to let her peek at some statistics graphs.

"I have summer school, remember?"

Of course she did. It was all part of the ten-year life plan Nicky mapped out one night during a sleepover. Keeley thought it was a joke until Nicky started taking courses at the community college. Even if Nicky couldn't help her study, maybe they could get together. Her social life had been pretty nonexistent this summer. "Well, what about getting dinner after? There's this little café on the pier I've been dying to try," Keeley suggested.

Nicky gave her an apologetic look. "I'm meeting with my study group. We're grabbing food on campus and then prepping for the final. Why don't you ask Zach? He'd go anywhere as long as there's food."

"He's getting dinner with the team." It was depressing knowing they both had plans while she had a whole lot of nothing. It felt like everyone was leaving her behind, and the worst part was they didn't even seem to notice.

"We'll get together after finals," Nicky promised.

The ride came to an end and a bittersweet feeling swept over Keeley. Summer was almost over and now she was going to be a senior in high school. It was exciting, but also terrifying. Her future was a big question mark and she had no answer.

Chapter 2

iWonder Who He Is

...

Later that night, she took Nicky's advice and cracked open the books. She hoped finishing an assignment would make her feel less like a loser who had nothing to do, but it took less than fifteen minutes before boredom set in. Promising herself to start tomorrow, she pushed the work to the other side of the bed and grabbed her laptop. Nothing cured boredom more than catching up on her favorite shows. About halfway through, her eyelids began to droop.

She didn't know how long she'd slept, but the ringing phone woke her up in seconds. Zach. The party. The redhead. Groggily, she answered, "The sex better have been worth waking me up for."

There was a slight pause. "Now that sounds like something I'd like to hear more about."

She blinked, then bolted upright. Squinting against the harsh light of the screen, she saw "Unknown Caller." Alarmed, she asked, "Who's this? Where's my brother?" Keeley's dog, Tucker, who was lying at the foot of the bed, popped his head up.

"I have no idea and frankly, I don't care."

"Then why are you calling me? And how'd you get this number?"

"I dialed it." An implied "duh" to his tone.

She was too tired to deal with this. She should hang up.

"Hello? Are you there? Or did I lose you?" The voice paused. "Look, I don't know what you're on and I'm not going to ask, because I live by a strict plausible deniability rule, but you have my phone and I want it back."

Was this guy for real? She twisted to see the clock on her nightstand. "First off, it's one in the morning. I'm not on anything except sleep, which, I'll point out, you rudely woke me up from. And second, I don't have your phone."

"Yeah, you do," he insisted.

"I don't."

"That phone in your hand is mine. Not yours. *Mine*," he said, enunciating every word.

This had to be a prank. "Did my brother put you up to this? Is he trying to get back at me?" Crisscrossing her legs, Keeley hunched forward and rested her elbows on her thighs. Wisps of bangs too short to fit in her ponytail fell around her face. "Unbelievable.

I don't know what his problem is." She'd given him a fair deal for those keys.

"Would you just look through my phone?" he asked, sounding tired.

She didn't feel an ounce of sympathy. Not when this guy was being so rude. "I want serious groveling after I prove —" She swallowed the rest of the sentence as a picture of a red race car glowed on the screen.

"You said something about groveling ...?"

She refused to let her embarrassment show. "Does this mean you have my phone?"

"Is your background a picture of a brown dog?"

"That's Tucker." He wagged his tail at the sound of his name. Dropping her head to her knees, she wondered how this had happened. Wait. "Were you at the fair tonight?"

"Damn. Any chance you hung out at the tables by the food?" he asked.

And she'd thought she was lucky when she found the phone. What a load of crap. She flopped onto her mountain of pillows with a grunt.

"You're not on the toilet right now, are you? Because if you are, I'm hanging up."

"What? No!" she cried, horrified by the thought. "I'm on my bed."

"In that case, I'm all ears. Don't leave anything out."

Typical guy. Zach's friends were all the same. "How do you know I'm not some eighty-year-old woman who has dentures and wears flannel?" she asked.

"There's no way your voice belongs to a little old lady. But fine, if you won't tell me what you're wearing, how about I tell you? Nothing but my lucky boxers, which seems fitting."

"How does it seem fitting?"

"I'm talking to you, aren't I?"

She smiled, even though she told herself not to. Man, this guy was shameless. Oddly enough, it made her want to respond in the same fashion.

"That got you, didn't it?" he asked. "Straight to the heart."

"No way," she lied.

He tsked. "Telling lies is a sin. I know I have a gift, especially when it comes to the ladies."

She rolled her eyes. "You're a cocky SOB, aren't you?"

"If by SOB, you mean sexually omnipotent boy. I am, for sure."

"Or a boy with sexually offensive behavior," Keeley countered.

"You know, you might want to rethink insulting the person who has your phone. Let's see, who can I prank call at one in the morning?" His voice sounded muffled. "Hmmm ... Nana? Uncle Tom? Cousin Louise?"

That was a bold move. He wouldn't dare ... would he? "Don't forget, I have your phone, too," she threatened.

"If you want to prank call people, be my guest. I'll even give you a list. Start with Marlene Baker. The girl refuses to leave me alone."

"I don't see why," she retorted. "I've been on the phone with you for five minutes and I have no desire to repeat the experience."

"Be nice, baby doll, or else," he warned.

"Or else what? And don't call me that."

18

"Then what should I call you?"

She hesitated. She knew nothing about this guy.

"Scared?" he asked. "I'll tell you my name if you tell me yours."

"I'm not scared," she protested. "Just cautious. You could be a serial killer or something. I don't even know how old you are."

"I'm in high school. How about you?"

"Same. I ..."

When it was clear she wasn't going to say more, he pointed out, "We're going to meet anyway to switch back our phones. What's the big deal?"

"You go first."

He sighed. "You always this difficult?"

"Now who's the one avoiding the question?"

A beat passed. Then another. "I'm Talon."

"That's unusual," she commented, not recognizing it. She wanted to ask for his last name, but then he would want to know hers, and when people in this town heard Brewer, they thought of Zach. As soon as they learned she was related to him, they launched into what a great player he was and asked a million questions about his plans for the future. It sucked that the most interesting thing about her was her brother.

"I told you mine. Now, what's yours?" he asked, ignoring her comment. "And don't think you can get out of it."

She wavered, still unsure about giving a complete stranger her name.

"Come on. Just tell me."

She swallowed. "It's Keeley."

He repeated her name under his breath. "It suits you."

She frowned. "How so?"

"It's a beautiful name for a beautiful voice," he declared. He sounded like a character out of a soap opera—dramatic and completely fake.

"Please stop. That's so lame."

"It's not lame," he grumbled, his voice back to normal.

"Beautiful name for a beautiful voice," she mocked.

"I don't sound like that. My voice is deeper, more masculine," he protested. "I—Hey! What's with the laughing?" But Keeley was too far gone to respond. "I'm going to hang up if you don't stop," he threatened.

"Wait, wait!" Keeley managed to say as she got her laughter under control. "I have a question."

"No, you don't. I'm going."

"I'm serious. I have a question."

"What?"

"Does that line"—she giggled, not being able to hold it back—"actually work?"

"Will you stop?!"

"Are you one of those guys who hits on girls at a shopping mall and uses lines like"—she deepened her voice—"'Do you come here often, baby?'"

Silence.

"Oh my God, you are!"

Talon didn't even bother responding as he hung up, leaving her with silence. She'd call him tomorrow and get her phone back. As she lay down, a little part of her wondered what he'd be like in person.

Chapter 3

iWill Not Beg

●●●

The next morning, Keeley woke to a shouting match between Zach and her parents. She sat on the second-floor landing, which overlooked the living room, and watched it all unfold. Zach, in the same clothes from yesterday, was on the couch with his arms crossed and a scowl on his face. Her mother was on a nearby chair, shaking her head in disappointment, while her father paced the living room.

"You could have gotten yourself killed!" her father roared.

"Dad —"

"What were you thinking?!" His face was blotchy and red.

"Dad —"

"Obviously you weren't, were you? You put yourself and everybody else on the road in danger!"

Zach slapped a hand against the suede armrest. "I said I was sorry. And I got home fine. Nothing bad happened!"

And everyone says he's the smart one in the family, Keeley thought.

Her father's face was purple now, his voice low and even. Somehow that was scarier than the yelling. "You're grounded for the next month. You can't leave the house except to go to practice."

Zach leapt to his feet. "You can't do that! I'm captain of the team. I'm supposed to help the incoming freshmen —"

"Then you should have thought of that before drinking and driving!"

So that's what the fight was about. Why didn't he call her?

"Mom, please," Zach begged. "Talk to him."

"I agree with your father. It's bad enough you were drinking, but to drive? You should be grateful we're letting you play football."

For a second, Zach looked like he was going to argue, but he shut his mouth and stalked up the stairs. He came to an abrupt halt when he caught sight of Keeley. "It's all your fault!" he hissed so their parents couldn't hear.

"What did I do?"

"You know exactly what. I thought we had each other's backs. Guess I was wrong, *twin.*"

The resentment in his voice made her stand. "I should be the one pissed off. What were you thinking?"

"What choice did I have? I was out past curfew. If Mom and Dad found out, they would have grounded me."

"You call me. You don't get behind the wheel."

"Are you serious? I call and text for an hour, and when I finally get through, you hang up on me."

He was full of crap. "Lie to Mom and Dad all you want, but don't lie to me. You probably wanted to impress that girl and —"

He shoved his phone in her face. Her name was displayed on every line of the call log, the time stamped between two and three a.m. Guilt hit her full force. "Zach, I —"

"Forget it," he scoffed and brushed past.

If something bad happened to him ...

The thought made her sick. "Wait, Zach." She grabbed his shoulder, but he shrugged her off. "I never got those," she called after him, but he didn't stop.

It was that boy. Talon. He was the reason Zach was mad. Rushing to her room, Keeley dialed her own phone — which he had — but it went to voice mail. Five seconds later, a text popped up.

Can't talk right now. Only text.

You hung up on my brother?!

He called at 2 a.m. Of course I hung up.

You should have told me. It was important.

More important than my beauty sleep?
I don't think so.

> I don't give a damn. He drove home drunk because he couldn't get a hold of me.

Not my problem.

> How could you not care? What if he got in an accident??

Why are you mad at me? Your bro is the one who drove drunk. Hasn't he heard of Uber?

Of course he'd heard of it. But it wasn't like he could use Uber when their parents got the monthly bill. They would spot the charge in an instant. Talon had no right to judge.

> What time are you free? We need to exchange our phones. The sooner, the better.

Can't. Left with my team for football camp today.

She must have read that wrong. Keeley blinked and then started to panic.

> Why didn't you tell me this yesterday? We could have met this morning.

Bet you wish you hadn't laughed at me now, huh?

She didn't have her phone because he wanted payback? Of all the stupid, selfish reasons. If her parents found out, they'd never buy her a phone again.

> What I wish is that you didn't exist. When are you coming back?

In a week.

> What am I supposed to do till then?!

Dream of me. Word on the street is I'm pretty impressive, if you know what I mean. 😉

She stared at the winking emoji. He was obnoxious, but she had to admit he was also a little funny. In that annoying I-want-to-smack-you kind of way.

> And I'm sure the hefty fee you paid some girl to say that was well worth it. I need my phone.

Stop worrying. We'll just forward the texts and voice mails till I return.

> Hell no! You've already proved you fail at that and there is no way I'm allowing you to go through my phone.

25

It's cute you think I already haven't. BTW, only 20 numbers? Pretty pathetic.

There was a knock on the door and then her mom came in. "Oh good. You're up. Breakfast is ready."

When she got to the dining room, Zach was sitting at the table. She tried to catch his eye so she could explain the whole Talon debacle, but he pointedly looked away. An ache formed, but she pushed it away. He wasn't ready to listen to her. That was fine. She'd try again later.

Her mom walked in with a stack of pancakes. "Aren't you going to sit?"

"Just seeing if we need syrup or anything," Keeley replied. Forcing a smile, she took her usual seat across from Zach.

Breakfast was uncomfortable. Zach acted like she had the plague or something. If she was reaching for pancakes, he made sure he was nowhere near the syrup. If she grabbed a sausage, his hands would suddenly be far away from the ketchup. It was ridiculous and it ate away at her. Keeley grabbed her plate and stood. "I'm done."

"You can leave that there. Zach's doing the dishes," her dad informed her.

"It's okay. I can —"

"Leave it," her dad ordered.

She glanced at Zach, but his eyes were glued to the tablecloth. She couldn't say anything, not with their parents there, so she set down the plate and went into the living room. Out of habit, she checked the phone for news from Nicky, but what she found was a flood of texts from Talon.

Did I hurt your feelings?

Still ignoring me?

99 bottles of beer on the wall, 99 bottles of beer. Take one down, pass it around, 98 bottles of beer on the wall.

98 bottles of beer on the wall, 98 bottles of beer. Take one down, pass it around, 97 bottles of beer on the wall.

97 bottles of beer on the wall, 97 bottles of beer ... I can do this all day you know.

She shook her head and scrolled through the other twenty texts saying the same thing.

You're like the song that never ends.

Where'd you go? I missed you.

Aren't you supposed to be playing football instead of annoying me?

I'm on a bus. 3 more hours till we reach camp which means I'm all yours. Only 77 bottles to go. 😊

There were at least seventy-seven other things she'd rather have than him. Zach talking to her, for starters.

Keeley jumped when her mom sank into the couch next to her. She quickly silenced the phone and flipped it over. Her mom would become suspicious if she saw that many texts, especially since they were coming from her own phone.

Her mom pushed some hair out of Keeley's face. "Is everything okay? Your dad and I noticed something was off at breakfast."

No matter what problems she had with Zach, she would never rat him out. "It's nothing to worry about."

"Was it about last night?"

"Seriously, Mom. It'll blow over. You know how Zach and I are. We fight and then make up five minutes later."

Her mom stayed put, clearly hoping Keeley would say more, but when Keeley didn't, she patted her knee. "Okay. Well, I'm here if you want to talk."

Keeley waited till she was out of the room before checking the phone. Twenty-one texts. It was a good thing she had unlimited messages.

56 bottles of beer on the wall, 56 bottles of beer. Take one down, pass it around, 55 bottles of beer on the wall.

Don't you have teammates you can go bother?

You know most girls would die for the chance to text with me.

Then go annoy them.

I can't. You have my phone, remember? I'm starting to think you have some serious memory issues.

My only issue is you. Since we're stuck with each other, I think we need to promise we'll forward each other texts and missed calls.

I already offered and you turned me down.

She scrolled through their texts. Crap. He was right. She'd been so upset about Zach that she blew him off when he suggested it.

I'm agreeing now.

You snooze, you lose, baby doll. Looks like I'm the one holding all the cards.

That's where he was wrong. He controlled her phone, but she controlled his.

If you don't forward all my texts, I won't forward yours.

That's fine.

Wait. What?

You don't care?

Already told my parents we'd have spotty reception so we're communicating via email.

But ... what about his friends? Then again, if he was anything like Zach, most of his friends were on the team. Damn it. Now what? She refused to beg.

Guess you'll have to think of another way to get me to agree. Flattery will get you everywhere. 😊

As if she would add to his ego. She'd rather eat dirt.

I am not that desperate and you're not that lucky.

I think you just threw down a challenge. Game on, Keeley. Game on.

The taunt left her angry. They were in this mess together. He should be helping instead of using her phone as leverage.

She needed to get out for a while. She thought about asking Nicky to the movies, but remembered she was in class. Instead she sent her two long voice mails, venting about Talon and Zach. Then she took Tucker to the park. Not that it made her feel any better. She had no solution about Talon, Zach was still mad at her, and she hadn't finished a single summer assignment. All in all, a crappy day.

That night she was in her room rereading one of her favorite books when she heard her brother. She rushed to the hallway, but he brushed past her and slammed the door to his room. Enough was enough. She'd never gone to bed angry at him, and she wasn't about to start now.

When she went in, Zach was on his bed, scribbling on a pad of paper. Diving right in, Keeley said, "Zach, I'm sorry about last night. I know you're mad, but I didn't miss your calls on purpose." There was a small hesitation in his writing so she took it as a good sign. "I guess you're working on the plays for tomorrow's scrimmage. Always Mr. Prepared," she joked, peeking at the paper. He angled away so she couldn't see. "Okay. Um, do you think you can drop me off at the library tomorrow on the way to your game?"

"It's not exactly on the way," he pointed out.

She was trying to be nice and he couldn't bother to do the same? "You really going to keep this up?"

"Keep what up?"

"Zach, I didn't get those calls last night. If I did, I would have picked you up. You know that."

He thrust his chin out. "I wasn't planning on drinking last night, but I did. And I thought it was okay because you promised you'd drive me home. You didn't. End of story."

She understood why he was upset, but he was acting like it was all her fault. "I'm sorry I missed your calls, and it sucks that you got grounded, but you chose to drive. No one forced you."

"Whatever. I need to finish this." He went back to his notepad.

She stood there awkwardly, staring at his back. "Okay, well ... good night, Zach."

His silence followed her back to her room.

Chapter 4

iHold the Cards

• • •

Talon's refusal to forward texts bothered her. She spent two days trying to think of something to force his hand but she had nothing. To make it worse, he kept texting her articles like "Twenty-Five Compliments for the Man You Love" and "Ten Ways to Say You're Sorry." More like ten ways to get his ass kicked.

"Hey, kiddo. What are you doing out here?" her dad asked, opening the screen door to the back patio.

She lifted her head from the hammock. "Just thinking."

He sat under the umbrella that was giving her shade. "And how's the homework coming? You going to finish before school starts?"

"I'm getting there," Keeley hedged. If he knew the truth, he wouldn't let her out of the house. Not that she had anywhere to go, but still.

"I know it's a lot of work, but these advanced assignments are getting you ready for senior year. And not only that, they'll look good on your transcript. Colleges love challenging coursework." College was a sore subject in her family. One that had her sweating. Keeley threw a toy for Tucker, hoping to distract her dad, but he asked, "Are you still set on going to the East Coast?"

"And if I am?"

His disappointment was obvious. "Zach's applying to West Coast colleges."

"Zach's applying to football colleges," she corrected. But she knew his number-one choice was a school three hours away, known for its football program. Many players got drafted after graduating.

"He wants to go to the same school as you."

Zach took her need to leave personally. He didn't understand it wasn't about him. It was about her. She loved this beach town, but she wanted to see what else was out there.

Her dad continued. "I'd feel better if you two were together."

"Dad, I can handle myself."

"It's not you I'm worried about," he confessed.

She was surprised. Everyone viewed her brother as the more capable twin. "Zach will be fine. He always is —"

"I'll be fine with what?" Zach asked as he came outside with a bag of chips. He'd just gotten back from football practice. His clothes were stained and his hair was dripping with sweat. When he got near her, he shook his head, getting her wet. Judging by the smug look on his face, he knew it, too, but she didn't care. It was the first real emotion he'd shown her in days.

"You'll be fine if Keeley goes to a different college," her dad told him.

Zach wasn't happy to hear that. "You still in that East Coast phase?"

"It's not a phase."

"It's stupid. No one picks a college based on location."

"You're picking solely on football!"

"That's different. I'm getting a scholarship for that."

"You don't have any offers yet," she pointed out.

"I will. And when I win the state championship this year, I'll get even more. Probably a full ride."

Out of the corner of her eye, she saw her dad turn hopeful. Their family wasn't rich by any means, but they weren't poor either. Was money a concern?

"You don't think I can do it?" Zach asked, taking her silence the wrong way. There was a flash of hurt in his eyes before it flickered away.

"I didn't say that."

"Yes, you did. How can you think —"

She interrupted, knowing her brother wouldn't shut up once he got started. "I know you can win. You're the best quarterback out there." Of course, she had no idea if that was true, but it was her sisterly duty to say it.

"Keeley, there's no harm in applying to multiple schools," her dad insisted. "Besides, you might not get into one back east."

"Hey! I can get in."

"Not with those SAT scores," her brother mused.

"They're not yours, but they aren't terrible either." Her reading and writing were fine, and there was still time to get up the math.

"I offered to study with you," Zach reminded her. It was a nice offer, if she wanted to get yelled at.

"There's nothing wrong with wanting to live somewhere else," she insisted, refusing to feel bad. Why did people act so surprised when she wanted to try something new? "And Dad, weren't you the one who told me to step out of my comfort zone?"

"I guess I did," he relented. "You're just going to have to let your old man sulk over losing you."

"You are pretty old," Zach said playfully.

"And your knees creak when you get up," Keeley added.

"And to think I wanted children," her dad grumbled, going back to the house.

When Zach didn't follow, she tossed him a tentative look. "So ..."

A few strands of hair fell in his eyes and he pushed them to the side. "I need to mow the lawn, so if you could move the hammock ..."

Disappointment struck. "Oh, sure. I was getting burned anyway." More strands fell as he helped move her things. "You need a haircut," she observed. He never let it grow this long. Zach liked to keep a clean-cut appearance. Total opposite of her style, which was casual and untucked.

"Thought I'd try something new."

She took a clip out of her own hair. "Here. This will help."

He gathered some strands and pinned them to the top of his head. "Tell anyone and you die."

"'Course not. Wouldn't want to ruin your precious rep," she teased.

"Hey, don't diss it. Reputation is important to a guy."

She wondered if that was true for everyone. Even someone like Talon. "That's it!" she exclaimed as an idea struck. "I don't know why I didn't think of it sooner." His reputation was the key. She needed to find dirt on him. What secrets was he hiding?

Back in her room, she grabbed Talon's phone and looked at his photo albums. For an arrogant guy, there weren't that many pictures. And absolutely none of himself or his friends. A particularly colorful picture caught her attention and she zoomed in. *Are those Peeps?* she thought, recognizing the marshmallow bird candies dusted with sugar. *Dressed as ... pirates?* They were in front of a backdrop drawing of a pirate ship and fighting each other with toothpicks. Flicking through the album, she saw more pictures like that, except the Peeps were dressed as other characters, like Luke Skywalker from *Star Wars*. They were ... cute. In a weird kind of way. Certainly not what she was expecting. And nothing she could use. Not when she didn't even know what those things were supposed to be.

Keeley looked through his music, but there were no embarrassing bands. She did note, however, his large selection of country music. That would explain the drawl in his voice. Next, she thumbed through his apps, but was dumbfounded. He didn't have any social media. Not even Instagram, or Twitter, or Snapchat. What was with this guy? It was like he was living in the dark ages.

His phone started ringing, and when she saw the name, she could hardly believe it. This could be the advantage she was looking for. "Is this ... Talon's mom?" she asked.

"Oh!" the woman exclaimed, seeming taken aback by the greeting. "Yes, I'm his momma, but you're not my son." Her voice was warm and inviting with a slight country twang to it.

"No, ma'am. My name's Keeley." Maybe it was the accent, but suddenly Keeley was using manners she didn't know she had.

"None of this 'ma'am' business," she kindly scolded. "I may be a mother, but I don't have any gray hairs yet. Call me Darlene, suga'."

Keeley wasn't sure what she'd expected, but it certainly wasn't this. "Yes, ma'a — I mean, Darlene," she corrected.

"Do you mind telling me why you're answering my son's phone? He's supposed to be at football camp."

Keeley quickly explained the mishap at the fair and how they switched phones.

"That's quite a predicament you two have gotten in. I wish he had given it to me. I could have met you and exchanged the phones myself. I wonder why he didn't tell me this before he left. Probably wanted to keep talking to you. Bet you're a pretty thing."

"I don't know about that." Keeley laughed. "Honestly, I think Talon just wanted to get back at me."

"Talon?" his mother questioned.

"Uh ... yes. You're Talon's mom, right?"

"I'm Talon's momma. Sorry, I thought you said something else. So, what is this about my son getting back at you?"

Keeley couldn't very well tell Darlene about that first phone call when she'd made fun of her son and called him an SOB. Instead, she lied and said, "It's nothing."

"That boy." Darlene sighed. "Just like his daddy. Always letting his emotions run wild. And he was so good growing up. What happened? Where did I go wrong?"

"Umm ..."

"He never brings his friends home or tells me what's happening in his life."

"Darlene —"

"And don't think I haven't noticed him fooling around with those girls. Coming home with lip gloss stains on his collar. I just don't know what to do anymore. It's like he doesn't want me around. He didn't even accept my Facebook friend request. You wouldn't do that to your mother, would you?"

"Uh ... I ..." Her mother couldn't even figure out how to access her cell phone's voice mails, much less Facebook. Thank God for small favors.

"Of course you wouldn't, suga'. I can tell. She's lucky." Darlene sniffed. "Do you know he forces me to sit in the back of the bleachers during his football games? Says he's embarrassed. My own son! I don't see why. It was just a Dolly Parton costume. It was almost Halloween."

Keeley cringed. She had to feel a little sorry for the guy, but this was exactly the type of information she needed in order to get his cooperation. She laughed like his mom had just told the best joke of all time. "I would have loved to see that."

"I can send you a picture, darlin'. Do you want me to text it to Talon's phone?"

"That would be perfect. Thank you!" said Keeley, feeling almost guilty. "Darlene, I have to go, but it was a pleasure talking to you."

"You too. Take care now."

While she waited for the picture, she sent Talon a text.

> Had the most interesting conversation with your mom. She likes to talk. A lot.

Let him stew on that for a while. Now she could see why Talon sent her all those articles. Goading was fun.

Keeley slapped a hand over her mouth when she saw Darlene's photo. It was bad. Really bad. Like a gaudy, over-the-top kind of bad. No wonder Talon was embarrassed. But Keeley had to admit Darlene wore her Dolly costume with confidence. She didn't think she could have done the same.

> What did my mother tell you?

> Hello?

> You there?

> What did she say?

It was fun to watch him squirm.

My, my. The mighty Talon taken down by his mom.

Keeley! What did she tell you?

She sent him Darlene's picture. His response was immediate.

You wouldn't.

Who holds all the cards now?

Fine. I'll pass on your texts and calls.

I knew you'd see it my way.

You're incredibly annoying and irritating, you know that?

Coming from you that's a compliment.

If you wanted a compliment, baby doll, all you had to do was ask. I'd be more than happy to provide.

I think you've provided enough. Your mom told me about all those lip gloss stains.

Jealous?

Instead of responding, she sent him an article — "Twelve Signs She's Just Not Into You."

Chapter 5

iTalk to a Dog

...

That night Keeley was fast asleep when an unfamiliar ringtone played in her ear. Eyes still closed, she reached under her pillow and grabbed the phone. "'Ello?"

"Your brother is annoying," Talon mumbled, his voice rough with sleep.

"Tell me something I don't know."

"Wants you to pick him up from some chick's house. Chloe-something-or-other."

"He's at another party?"

"Said he snuck out with one of his buddies." What was Zach thinking? He was grounded. There would be hell to pay if their parents caught him. They'd all but threatened to take him off the football team if he broke another rule.

She rolled out of bed, reached into her closet and grabbed the first thing she could find — a blue Edgewood High sweatshirt. It clashed with her orange polka-dot pajama shorts, but she was too tired to care. She went to slip on her flip-flops, but they were gone. Tucker must have buried them in the backyard again. All she could find were the rain boots her father had given her for Christmas last year. She slipped them on, then crept past her parents' room and down the stairs.

"You still there?" she whispered. "What time is it?"

"Two thirty. Why is he even calling you?"

"He's drunk."

"So?"

"He can't drive."

"Let me get this straight. He calls and you drop everything to help him out?"

She frowned at his tone. "I'm his sister. Wouldn't you do the same?"

"He got into the situation. He can get himself out."

Keeley grabbed her car keys off the kitchen table and tiptoed to the front door. "You're an only child, aren't you?"

"That's irrelevant. You need to stop acting like his personal chauffeur and show him some tough love."

"I'm not —" Tucker rushed after her, thinking he was going for a walk. He whined when she opened the door, pushing himself in between her legs. Shushing him, she glanced up the stairwell to see if her parents had woken up. Their room stayed dark, so she waved Tucker away. "Go to my room," she ordered quietly.

"I thought you'd never ask," Talon replied. "I knew all that protest was just an act. No one can refuse my charm."

"I was talking to the dog," she hissed as she silently closed the door and hurried to her car. "Although there is an uncanny resemblance."

"And how would you know? You've never seen me."

"Maybe not physically, but personality-wise. I mean you both love to chase and you sulk like children when your favorite toy gets taken away. Not to mention needing constant attention and stroking."

"You're right. I need lots of stroking."

"I'm talking about your ego, pervert."

Talon laughed. Unbelievable.

"Shut up, dude!" a voice yelled in the background. Talon must have covered the phone with his hand because all Keeley could hear was a few muffled noises. There was some white noise, then Keeley heard a door close.

She hesitated before asking, "Talon?"

"Sorry, my roommate's being an ass and kicked me out."

"I'm surprised you let him." Talon didn't seem the type to let himself be pushed around. Keeley turned on the car and switched him to speakerphone. She pulled out of the driveway and waited until she was at the end of the street before turning on the headlights.

"Coach is doubling up practices so everyone's exhausted."

"You should get some sleep then."

"I'm not that tired. Besides, I'm talking to you."

"So, I'm your shot of caffeine?" she teased. She froze when she realized how flirty that sounded. In fact, the whole conversation had a playful undertone. She wasn't sure how she felt about it.

"Something like that," he replied. "Explain to me again why you're always running to the rescue. What does your brother have over you?"

"Nothing! I do it because I have his back, and he has mine."

"What has he done for you?"

"Why do you care? It's not like it affects you," she replied.

"I'm curious."

"And curiosity killed the cat."

"Good thing I'm a dog then, huh?"

His answer was so unexpected she found herself cracking up. "Well, at least you admit it."

She parked a couple houses down from Chloe's house. "As stimulating as this conversation is, I have to go."

"You there already?"

"Unfortunately," she sighed, sidestepping a pile of puke on the sidewalk. She hated going to parties like this, where everyone was drunk and sloppy.

"You don't sound too thrilled. I completely understand."

"You do?"

"Of course. I wouldn't be thrilled to say goodbye to me either."

She rolled her eyes. "Good night, Talon."

"Don't miss me too much."

After hanging up, Keeley hopped around the red plastic cups littering the entryway and poked her head into the family room.

Several couples were making out on the couches and chairs. She raised an eyebrow at one particular pair: Randy, her ex, and Allison Lineberry, the captain of the girls' soccer team.

"Keeley!" She looked over to see Cort, Zach's best friend, stumbling toward her. Her hands automatically reached out to steady him. "What're ya doing here?" he yelled over the music.

"Looking for Zach," she told him, taking in a whiff of beer and rum. Cort placed both hands on her shoulders and laughed. "What?" she asked.

"You look funny," he said, eyeing her up and down.

Right. Her rain boots and polka-dot PJs. She completely forgot. But she wasn't there to impress anyone. Keeley held her chin up and said, "Thanks. So have you seen Zach?"

Cort pulled her into the kitchen and pushed her in front of a group of football players. "Look who's here," he announced, showing her off like a carnival prize.

"Keeley!" they greeted her, shouting like they were at a concert instead of a house. She lifted a hand in a silent hello. These kids had been to her house countless times over the past three years. Cort shoved a red cup at her, but Keeley didn't take a sip.

"Did ya see Randy?" he asked.

"Hard not to." Just seeing him had brought back a flood of memories from when they were dating. He'd been easy to talk to and fun to be around, until they started hanging out with his friends. Then he started pressuring her to attend parties and told crude jokes that shocked her. When they were alone, he was different again, so Keeley stuck with him. But then one night, she overheard his friends trash-talking her, and Randy didn't say a single word to defend her. She ended it the next day. But she still thought about it. *What is wrong with him?* she wondered. And what's wrong with her?

"Dude, football is going to dominate this year!" someone yelled. As usual, the mention of football caught everyone's attention.

"Edgewood for the win!"

"This year is going to be epic!"

Keeley had to find Zach and get out of there. Things could get crazy once they got going.

The guys started gathering, so she scooted out of the way. She felt awkward and out of place as they slapped each other on the back and shouted some chant she'd never heard.

"Edgewood is going to crush Crosswell!" Cort yelled, throwing both hands up and sloshing beer all over himself. A cheer of approval rang out. The Edgewood-Crosswell rivalry was legendary. No one knew how it started or why, but it didn't matter. The biggest event of the year was the annual football face-off between the schools.

"Did I hear something about crushing Crosswell?" A smiling Randy strutted into the kitchen with Allison. "Because I'll drink to that." His smile faded when he caught sight of Keeley. "I didn't know you were coming."

He'd been a little preoccupied, Keeley thought.

"I'm here because Zach called. Does anyone know where he is?" Keeley asked.

Allison smiled sheepishly. "He's with Gavin."

"Who?"

Cort looked down at her. "His little buddy. You know, the freshman he got paired with." It was tradition that freshman football players were assigned to a senior teammate. It was supposed to be a mentoring program, but the football players used it as a way to get their cars clean and have someone fetch them lunch.

"Keels! There you are," Zach said with a goofy grin. His cheeks were flushed and his eyes red. Then he picked her up and spun around. It was the nicest he'd been since their fight.

She forced him to put her down when she became dizzy. "You ready to go?"

"Not till you meet my little guy." Zach snapped his fingers in the air and motioned for a boy with sandy hair to come forward. He was the same height as her brother, but without the muscle and weight. He looked more like a long-distance runner than a football player. "Keels, this is Gavin. Gavin, my twin sister, Keeley."

"Hey, there," she said, noticing his hunched shoulders and averted eyes.

He mumbled something that barely resembled a "hello" and then backed away. Zach shook his head and then gave a long, drawn-out sigh that had Gavin turning red. Keeley felt a wave of sympathy for him. Poor kid was going to get murdered on the field if he couldn't even handle her brother.

As they headed out, a thought occurred to her. "Does Gavin need a ride?"

Zach scrunched up his eyes and swayed. "I'm sure he's good. There are plenty of people he can hitch a ride with."

"Then why didn't you do the same?" She could still be asleep in bed.

"You're here ..."

"Yeah, but I shouldn't be," Keeley muttered to herself, sliding into the car. As she drove home, she turned on a radio station they both liked. But when Zach's favorite song started playing and he didn't sing along, she knew something was up. Turning the volume down, she said, "All right. What's wrong?" Had he overheard her comment? She didn't want to fight again.

He sent her a furtive look. "Nothing."

Her worry lifted. If he were mad at her, he would have said so. "Tell me. I want to know."

"I can't. I don't want you to be mad. Promise you won't be mad."

"I'll try not to be," she said, growing wary. Had he done something when he was too drunk to know any better?

He swallowed, then confessed. "I got you an interview and tour of Barnett next week." Barnett University was known for three things: beautiful beaches, high SAT scores and football. None of which interested Keeley. Why on earth would he do this? "This is why I kept it a secret!" he said, motioning to her face.

Was he really that surprised? He went behind her back! She felt her blood racing. Why did he think he knew what was best for her?

Zach rushed on. "I know you don't want to go there, but listen. I was talking to one of their football recruiters, and he said they have great programs for incoming freshmen who don't know what they want to major in. They set you up with a bunch of different courses so you can see what you like."

"I have no clue where I want to go," said Keeley. Barnett wasn't on her list. It wasn't off her list either, but she wanted to be the one making the decision. Not her brother.

"You could at least visit and take the tour. You never know. You might really like the place," he coaxed.

She remembered the relief in her dad's face when Zach mentioned his potential scholarship. A California college would be cheaper: in-state tuition.

"Come on, Keels. I put in a lot of effort to get this. They were all booked but I begged the recruiter. And I even got you an extra spot so you could take someone with you —"

"Like Nicky," she suggested. He'd meant himself, but that wasn't happening. Besides, he'd already toured Barnett. He didn't need to go again.

"Of course," he said, scowling. For some reason, he wasn't Nicky's biggest fan.

"What's your deal with her?"

"Nothing. So you'll go to Barnett? Take a look around?" he pressed.

"Fine. I'll go." If it would make him stop bugging her about colleges. She needed this to end, now.

Zach pointed out his window. "Burgers! Let's stop. I'm starving."

"I hate going here. The car reeks afterward."

"But I'm hungry. And you don't use the car that much anyway." Zach tapped her shoulder. "Come on, come on. Let's go!"

Keeley turned off the street toward the parking lot. Then she realized there could be room for ... negotiation. "How's this — I'll pull over for burgers if you give me the car for the rest of the month." August was almost over but it didn't matter. She was realizing she couldn't let Zach push her around all the time. He was taking her willingness to say yes for granted. Much as she hated to admit it, Talon — a complete stranger — had been right.

"No. Hell no. I need it for football practice," said Zach.

"Get Cort or one of your buddies to take you. There's no reason you can't bum a ride off them."

"How would it look if the captain of the team had to beg for a ride?"

"I doubt you would have to beg." Zach had more friends than he knew what to do with.

"These kids look up to me. I need to be a good leader and show them —"

"You left Gavin to fend for himself!"

Changing tactics, he softened. "You know how important football is to me, Keels. I've worked hard get where I am."

"Then I guess you're not getting any food." She rolled down a window and let the smell of salty fries waft in.

He clutched his stomach as it growled. "Fine. You can have the car. Since when did you become so underhanded and mean?"

She considered for a moment. "Since I started talking to a dog."

"Huh?"

She just smiled and pulled into the drive-through.

Chapter 6

iHave an Idea

•••

The house was quiet as Keeley finished up her English paper. She felt good about what she'd accomplished, but then she saw the stack of assignments she still had left. She could ask Zach for help, but he was still sleeping. She took a quick break to grab some water and check her texts.

Did you get your brother home safe and sound last night? Tuck him in and read a bedtime story?

Your comments are so not appreciated.

I'll take that as a yes. If I call, will you tuck me into bed too?

Is there a reason you're texting me?

I think all that pent-up jealousy is really getting to you but don't worry, no other girl can compare to what I have with you.

That's your first mistake — thinking other girls can compare.

She reread her text. Most people didn't see this side of her. Normally, it took time for her to feel comfortable bantering back and forth, but with Talon, it was different. Texting had allowed them to sidestep the awkward getting-to-know-you phase.

And what's my second?

Letting your ego do all the talking.

Ouch. At least you didn't deny the jealousy.

She shook her head and put the phone down. Her gaze landed on the Barnett tickets Zach had given her last night. She hadn't understood why she would need them for a campus tour, but after seeing them, she realized why they were special. They admitted her and a friend to an exclusive event with the faculty and, more importantly, the admissions office. It was a great way to see the place, for sure, but also to schmooze the staff.

Keeley picked up the phone and called Nicky. She was expecting voice mail, so she was shocked when Nicky answered.

"Zach got me this tour of Barnett and I was wondering if you wanted to come." She told Nicky the dates. "It would be an overnight thing."

"I wish you'd told me sooner! My mom booked us at a spa for next weekend. It's my gift for studying so hard this summer."

That was a shame. Keeley could go by herself, she figured, but it would be a lot less fun.

"When are you getting your phone back?" asked Nicky. "Because I was going to call you, but I wasn't sure what number to use."

"I won't have it back for a few days."

"That sucks. How are things with that guy — Tim or something? Is he still driving you nuts?"

"Talon. And doesn't he always?" Keeley joked. "You won't believe who I talked to the other day — his mother!" Keeley launched into the story, making Nicky crack up. "I can hold that photo over his head till the end of time."

There was rustling in the background. Then Nicky said, "Listen, I have to go. I'm meeting my study group, but I promise I'll text you when I get home."

Keeley had heard that promise before, so she didn't believe it. At this point, Talon talked to her more than Nicky. Maybe things would change when they finally went back to school. She hoped so. She was getting sick of leaving voice mails.

Keeley hit the books for the rest of the day, getting through all her history and economics homework. All that was left was math. She was in her room when Talon rang.

"Randy called you," he told her.

Keeley froze. Her ex-boyfriend? "What does he want?"

Talon's voice turned mocking. "I'm guessing you guys dated ..."

"For a while."

"Well, he heard you were going to Barnett next week and was looking to score an invite."

How did Randy know about her extra ticket? Oh right ... Zach and his big mouth.

"I hope you two are over, baby doll. I told him he couldn't have the ticket because you gave it to me."

"You what?!" He lied to a complete stranger. Although she shouldn't be surprised. He never missed a chance to mess with her.

"And I might have alluded that since meeting me, you've gained an unhealthy obsession with all things Talon."

She should be furious, but his response was so ridiculous she couldn't help but be amused. Besides, it was Randy. Not like they were going to get back together. However, Talon didn't know that. "Why would you do that? For all you know, he was the love of my life."

"No guy would back off that quickly if he was in love."

Interesting. "So, if you were in love with a girl, you would have kept texting?"

There was a long pause. She'd surprised him. Good. Because she'd surprised herself. The idea of him in love ... it seemed unfathomable.

"Never mind," she said when the silence grew awkward.

"No, it's okay. I had to think about it for a second."

"I was just curious," she rushed to explain.

"I just ... I guess I've never thought of it before."

"Because you can't imagine falling in love?" The question popped out of nowhere.

"No, because I can't imagine a girl turning me down."

Of course he would take it as a joke.

There was noise in the background, then Talon said, "Hey, is your brother going to be calling in the middle of the night again?"

"Technically, he's grounded so he shouldn't call. Why?"

"My roommate was pissed when your brother called so late. I thought you could give him my number instead."

She hadn't even considered Talon's situation. "I'm sorry. I feel like a jerk."

"I bribed him with some sports drinks and cookies. It's fine." Talon changed the subject. "So you want to go to Barnett, huh?"

She looked down at the tickets. "Not really. I have my heart set on an East Coast school."

"I'm applying to some East Coast colleges, too. Try something different. Although, I don't know how I'd deal with those winters. *Brrr!*" he joked.

Finally, someone who got her! It was a relief to know she wasn't the only one. "I know, right? But it'd be an adventure."

"What schools are you thinking about? I have a couple in New York, Pennsylvania and Massachusetts."

Her ears grew hot. She hadn't even started researching. "I'm still working on my list."

"You have time. Applications aren't due till winter. So why visit Barnett then? Seems like a waste."

"My brother got the tickets. He's pressuring me to stay here so we can be close."

"Dude, he sounds like a leech. Can't he be without you for five minutes?"

"He's not like that. I know it sounds bad, but you don't know him like I do."

"Then explain it to me."

"He's ... well, he's —" It was hard to put in words what her brother was. He was stubborn, yet loyal. He could also be spontaneous when he wanted to be, but that didn't happen often. She blamed football. He was blind to everything else.

"Sounds like an exciting guy," Talon commented.

Keeley couldn't believe she was about to tell her story to a perfect stranger, but somehow Talon felt like more than that now. "It's like this, okay? One day, when we were little, our dad took us to the fair. There was a Batman eraser Zach wanted at one of the booths. It was a prize, at that game where you try to knock over a pyramid of bottles? Anyway, Zach tried again and again but he kept losing. Our dad offered to win it for him, but Zach refused. He wanted to be the one." He was so small, he could barely see over the booth. She remembered the frustration on his face, then the glint of determination when their dad said he should give up. "But he did it. He never gave up and he knocked down all the bottles and won."

"All that over an eraser?"

"Don't make fun of him," she threatened. She admired her

brother's focus. And that eraser meant more to her than Talon could ever know. During their first day of kindergarten, she had been terrified because she was going to be separated from Zach for the first time. He gave her that eraser, claiming it had magical powers to protect her. "He isn't perfect, but he's my brother. No one, and I mean no one, gets to make fun of him."

"I get it," Talon said, his voice subdued. "I mean, I'm an only child so I don't fully understand, but okay. I'm actually kind of jealous."

Keeley was surprised he admitted that. "What about your parents? Are you close to them?"

There was a short pause. "We're close but not like that."

There was a stretch of silence. She didn't want the conversation to end, so she said the first thing that popped in her mind. "I hate math. I think it was put on this earth to torture me. What's the point, you know?"

If he was surprised by the change, he didn't show it. "I think it's pretty useful."

"Really? I'm taking AP stats and the teacher assigned us a year's worth of problems this summer. I don't see how plotting a graph is going to help me in the future."

"You're taking AP classes?"

"You don't have to sound so surprised."

"I'm in some AP classes, too. But at my school, we take stats our junior year, not senior. I can help if you want," he offered. "I just finished the class last year."

She'd take all the help she could get. "Do you have time?"

"Yeah. The guys are watching a movie, but I've already seen it."

She knew team bonding was important. Zach was adamant about it. "It's fine. I don't want you to miss out."

"Nah. It's a stupid movie. I planned to skip it anyway."

"If you're sure ..."

"Baby doll, do I say stuff I don't mean?"

She huffed out a laugh. "No."

"There you go. Now, what's the problem?"

For the next hour, he actually helped her through her problems. She kept expecting him to get bored and leave, but he didn't. She couldn't believe it when they were done. They'd completed the whole assignment. "We did it! I thought it'd take me days to finish."

"I told you it wasn't that hard."

That wasn't true, Keeley thought. Statistics *was* hard. He was the reason it was easy. "You explained it so I actually understood the steps. No one's been able to do that before."

"All in a day's work," he joked. "It was fun."

"Let's not go that far."

"It couldn't have been that awful. You were laughing."

"Because you kept singing the formulas and made me sing along, too!"

"It helped you remember, didn't it? There's a method to my madness."

Keeley knew this was crazy, maybe even dangerous, but she had an idea. "Do you want to go to Barnett with me?" If he could make math enjoyable, maybe he could make a college tour fun as well. And there was no pressure to pretend like she cared, because he wasn't interested in Barnett either.

A startled silence. "Is this a serious offer?"

"Dead serious. The tour's coming up soon."

"And it would just be the two of us?"

Suddenly, she realized how the invitation sounded. It was forward. Very forward. But she didn't regret it either. "Well, us and the rest of Barnett. But if you don't want to go, no biggie."

"No. I think it would be fun. I look forward to it."

Interestingly enough, now she did, too.

Chapter 7

iMake a Friend

...

Two days later, Keeley shuffled into Nicky's house with two duffels and a sleeping bag. She dropped the bags to the ground and rotated her shoulders. "That feels so good. I brought hair, makeup and my entire nail polish collection. I couldn't narrow it down."

Nicky clapped her hands. "I'm so excited for Monday. First day of school is always the best. We have to look killer. Never know who's going to be in our classes."

Keeley lined up the nail polishes on the coffee table. "Hopefully we'll have classes together. Last year sucked. I love that you went to the office and complained."

"No harm in trying, right?"

Keeley held up the pale pink and the navy blue. "Which one? I plan on wearing my jeans and that blue tank Mom got me for my birthday."

"You always wear that. You should dress up a little. Wait. I have the perfect skirt for you." Nicky showed her a white floral skirt. "Before you say no, you could wear it with some sneakers to make it less fancy."

It wasn't her, but it was cute. And the beginning of a school year was the perfect time to try something different. "Okay, let's do it."

While they were painting their nails, Nicky confided about one of the guys in her study group. "He totally sees me as a little sister. It sucks. He's smart and hot and everything I want in a guy. I'm in love and I don't know what to do."

Keeley couldn't take her seriously. "You say that about a different guy every month."

"I'm not that bad," protested Nicky.

"What about Alec Davidson? You were convinced you were soul mates till he came out as gay. And remember David Gaston? You thought he was the 'one,' so we volunteered at the animal shelter ... and so did his girlfriend."

"Okay, okay!" Nicky interrupted. "I admit I may have been a little boy obsessed, but I'm older now. Wiser."

"And you have polish on your cheek." Keeley giggled.

Sheepishly, Nicky wiped it off. "So what about you? Any summer crushes?"

Keeley thought of Talon. Then shook her head. "I'm barely leaving the house," she complained. "Well, I'm driving Zach but that doesn't count."

"I still don't get why you bail him out so much."

"Not you, too," Keeley muttered, slumping down. "You sound exactly like Talon."

"It's a valid question." Nicky stretched out on the couch. "Speaking of Talon, I bet you'll be happy to get rid of his phone. Tomorrow's the day, right? Have you guys set up a time and place?"

She didn't know what she was feeling but it wasn't happy. She was used to talking to Talon every day. Would that disappear when they switched back phones? "We're going to meet at Java Hut. I don't know what time, though. I texted him this morning, but he has practice till five and then dinner at six, so I probably won't hear from him till later."

Nicky raised an eyebrow. "You know his schedule?"

Keeley flushed. "We've been forwarding texts and voice mails all week. Of course I know his schedule."

She knew a whole lot more than just his schedule. She knew he was a math wizard. That he loved old Western movies. She knew what made him laugh on YouTube and that he told really corny knock-knock jokes. And judging from the number of texts he got, Keeley was pretty sure he talked to her more than to his friends. She was trying to convince herself this was normal.

"I'll be happy when you get your phone back from him. Feels like we haven't talked in forever," Nicky grumbled.

Keeley knew it wasn't Talon's fault, or his phone's. Nicky was just too busy with her other plans. Luckily, a text from Talon kept her from having to respond. Very carefully, she tapped the screen so her nails wouldn't get messed.

I'm bored. Tell me a joke.

Did you get my text about meeting up tomorrow?

Java Hut @1 is good for me. Now tell me a joke.

Not everything is about you.

That's not a joke. Fine. I'll tell you one.

If you already know a joke, then why are you asking me for one?

Knock, knock.

Knowing he wouldn't budge, she played along.

Who's there?

Honey Bee.

Honey Bee who?

Honey Bee a dear and tell me a knock-knock joke.

She giggled, and Nicky glanced over. Why did she feel like she'd been caught? "Talon," she explained apologetically. A small wrinkle appeared between Nicky's brows as she continued painting.

You really do have a one-track mind.

I'm waiting …

Hey you wanna switch to calling instead?
I don't have afternoon practice.

I'm at the BFF's house.

I'm more fun to talk to.

He was fun but she couldn't let him know that.

Too bad there isn't a vaccine against narcissism. I think it's just what you need.

It was a good thing Nicky couldn't see these texts. She'd be shocked. Keeley never acted like this. Not even with Randy.

How can you be sure I have anything?
I'd be happy to strip down so you can perform a complete examination.

No need. I already know what my diagnosis would be. You suffer from Enhanced Genetic Obtuseness. Otherwise known as EGO. The symptoms include delusions of grandeur, lack of intelligence and an overabundance of confidence.

Ha! And what do you prescribe for this condition? Is there a cure?

Acute cases like yours need immediate treatment. I think a dose of reality and a shot of humility should do the trick.

If I agree, do I get you as my personal doctor?

She bit her lower lip, trying to stop the goofy grin from spreading.

Depends.

On what?

If you'll behave.

"You know, for someone who claims to hate Talon so much, you sure like talking to him," Nicky remarked.

"I don't hate him."

"Since when? All I've heard you do is complain." All Nicky heard were voice mails, and Keeley hadn't left one in days.

"He's not that bad," Keeley found herself saying. "He can be funny."

"If you say so." Her brown eyes glinted as she gazed at the phone in Keeley's hands. "Do you want to go to the pier with me after you switch phones? I have some extra tokens from the arcade."

"When did you go to the arcade?" Keeley had thought her friend was too busy to have fun.

"I don't know. Couple days ago, I guess. I was with my study group and we decided to blow off some steam."

Keeley's immediate thought was no. She didn't want to limit her meeting with Talon. But she hadn't seen much of Nicky, and Nicky's expression was so hopeful ... "Uh. Sure. We can do that."

A wide smile spread across Nicky's face. Then a text from Talon lit up the phone, and Nicky's lips flattened as she turned her attention back to her nails. Was she jealous? She had no right! Not after blowing her off all summer. Keeley gazed at the skirt Nicky was lending her. Maybe Nicky had a point. Tonight was supposed to be about them. About senior year. Keeley stashed the phone under her chair so she wouldn't be tempted to text.

When they finished painting, she and Nicky binge-watched a string of movies until they couldn't keep their eyes open. Then, just as Keeley was about to drift off to sleep, a buzzing noise woke her up. Her phone was vibrating. Talon. Since Nicky was curled under the covers, snoring, Keeley lifted the blankets and rolled out.

"Hey," she answered in a soft whisper. "What's up? Is something wrong?"

"I couldn't sleep. Thought I'd see if you were awake."

"Hold on." She carefully got to her feet, glanced at Nicky again and padded to the bathroom. Closing the bathroom door, she leaned her hip against the sink. "What's going on?"

"Nothing. I'm sorry. I shouldn't have called you," he said, his voice strained.

"No," she rushed on, fearing he would hang up. "I don't mind. I was in bed."

"I didn't mean to wake you."

"You didn't. I wasn't sleeping yet."

"I should let you go ..."

"Talon, when I say I don't mind, I mean I don't mind. So what's going on?"

"You know you're too nice for your own good. That's why people take advantage of you."

"I know something's bothering you." She could just tell.

"I just ... I ..."

"Hey," she said gently. A need to comfort him took hold. "You can tell me. Seriously."

"It's not — I just don't think I can ..."

It was obvious he wasn't ready to tell her. She changed the subject, going on and on about her night with Nicky. He seemed more relaxed, but his tone changed when she said, "Hey, I have a question for you."

"What?" he asked warily.

She'd been meaning to ask for a while. "What's up with the pictures on your phone? You know, those weird Peep things that are dressed up as characters."

"You mean the Peep-O-Ramas?"

"The Peep-a-what?"

"Peep-O-Ramas. They're dioramas made of Peeps."

"Wait. This is actually a thing?" She thought he was joking.

"Yeah, there's a yearly contest and everything."

"And you have this on your phone, why ...?"

"Because Peeps are possibly the greatest invention in human existence."

Keeley didn't quite agree. "They're not even the best candy."

"You know what? I don't think we can be friends anymore."

"I didn't know we *were* friends."

"Keeley, I've been through your phone. To some people, that's as good as being married."

She laughed at that. "Okay. So we're ... friends."

"I'll have you know that being my friend is an honor. One I don't bestow on many people."

"Please. I've seen your phone, too. You're friends with more people than I even know."

He made a scoffing sound. "Those aren't real friends. They're more like people I'm forced to know because of football. I'm talking about the people you call when you need someone to vent to."

"So if your teammates aren't your real friends, then who is?"

For a couple seconds, all she heard was him breathing. Then, in a quiet voice, he admitted, "Honestly, no one here. I had better friends back in Texas."

That explained something. "Texas, huh? I thought you had an accent."

"Yup. Born and raised. I moved here the summer before freshman year."

"I bet California was a huge change."

"You have no idea. I'm used to it now and I love being so close to the beach, but I miss the wide-open space. And the barbecue. God, I miss the barbecue."

"Why did you move?"

"My dad took a new job out here. He wanted to live someplace different. Plus, we have family 'round here."

"But you didn't want to go?" she asked. She was pretty sure she knew the answer.

He gave a short bark of laughter. "No, I sure as hell didn't. I wanted to stay, but after Gramps passed, the farm went to my dad. He didn't want to pay for the upkeep so he sold. Gramps promised it would be passed down to me. It was my inheritance. My dad had no right to sell." Anger infused his words. "He said the taxes were too expensive. But you know what? He didn't even try to come up with the money."

"I'm sorry," Keeley said, not knowing what else to say.

"I didn't mean to go off like that. I —"

"It's okay. I'd be upset, too." Was this why'd he called her?

"Yeah." The one word said it all. "Ma wanted to stay, too, but once Dad gets an idea in his head, he won't budge."

"Your mom is hilarious."

He groaned. "You don't have to live with her. I love her. It's just that she's a little ..."

"Over the top?" She suppressed the urge to yawn and hopped on the sink's counter, resting her back against the medicine cabinet.

"She still makes me school lunches. She even has a rotation of lunch boxes. You know, those square metal ones with the handles? Yeah, she uses those. Puts little notes inside with a juice box and a PB&J in the shape of a dinosaur. Won't stop doing it. So I eat the sandwich on my way home from school so she doesn't find out the box never leaves my car."

It was sweet he didn't throw the sandwich away. "So do you plan on going back to Texas?"

"I'm hoping after college I can move back permanently. But you never know. Life's weird like that."

Her eyelids were getting heavy, and a jaw-popping yawn escaped. "I better go."

Her yawn set off his own. "Yeah, me too."

She slid off the counter and said good night. Before she could hang up, he called out, "Hey, Keeley?"

"Yeah?"

His voice suddenly became rough. "I ... uh ... thanks."

"Did it help?"

"Yeah."

A rush of satisfaction warmed her. Then she said a first for them. "I'll see you tomorrow."

She could almost hear the smile in his voice. "Tomorrow."

Chapter 8

iMeet Him

...

Keeley was sweating as she drove to Java Hut. She turned up the air-conditioning but nothing helped. *God,* she thought, *I'm a wreck.* She wiped her palms on the steering wheel and ordered herself to calm down. After parking the car, she grabbed a tissue from her purse and dabbed her face and underarms. She could just drop the phone off at the front counter. Have an employee give the phone to Talon and keep hers until she could pick it up some other day. *Except that would be pathetic,* she told herself. Gathering what little courage she had, Keeley took a deep breath and went inside.

She fiddled with the ends of her shoulder-length hair, pulling and twisting as she scouted the area, but she was pretty sure he wasn't here. Needing something to do, she walked up to the counter. "A small iced coffee, please." She handed the employee her card and waited while he rung her up.

"They'll call your name when it's ready," he said.

Keeley grabbed an open seat. She checked the phone, but no text. She didn't want to seem like a loser, so she played a car racing game on his phone. It was pretty good. She'd have to tell Zach about it. Then, there it was:

I'm here.

A tall, blond boy was coming through the door. Even from a distance, Keeley could tell he was an athlete. He turned around, like he was looking for someone. He had high cheekbones, a strong jaw line and full lips. Almost perfect, except for a slight bend in his nose, like it had been broken.

"Keeley! Your order is up!" a voice cried out from behind the counter.

At the sound of her name, Talon snapped his head around. His eyes tracked her to the counter, where she picked up her drink. Feeling self-conscious, she lingered, taking an inordinate amount of time to add a straw, pretending she didn't see him.

"Hello, baby doll."

She'd recognize that voice anywhere. Deep tones with a slight drawl. Bracing herself, she turned around. His eyes were absolutely stunning. A vivid, cobalt blue that shimmered in the light.

He broke out in a grin. "You're not what I expected."

A customer bumped into her as he tried to reach the counter. Talon took hold of her arm and moved her to the side. "Let's get out of the way. Where's your table?" For some reason, her mouth wasn't working, but it didn't matter. He was so tall, he could easily see over the crowd. "Never mind. I see it," he said, pulling her along to the table against the window. It gave a perfect view of the beach and the pier jutting out into the water.

She wasn't usually this awkward. Moving to take a sip from her drink, she completely missed the straw. Talk about cringeworthy. And she wished she'd taken more time with her appearance. Her jeans and top were nothing special and she wore no makeup. It was a deliberate choice. One to remind both of them that this was no big deal. Just like any other day. But being here, looking in his eyes ... it didn't feel normal at all.

"I thought you were going to be more the girl-next-door type. Not so ..." She frowned, and he didn't finish his sentence. A slow smile reached his eyes. "I like it. You can stop looking like you want to punch me."

He leaned back in his chair and sprawled out his legs like she'd seen her brother do a million times. It always bothered her with Zach because he ate up all the free space, but it was different with Talon.

"No response? That's not like you," he said.

It wasn't. But she was speechless.

He reached over the table. "Thanks for getting this for me. You're a peach." Ignoring her confused look, he grabbed her drink and took a long sip. He added a satisfied sound at the end with an exaggerated wink.

It was the wink that jolted Keeley back. "Listen, Talon," she began, fingers drumming against the table. "Not everything revolves around you. You can't just —"

"There you are," he interrupted, his knee grazing hers. "I was wondering if I had the right girl, but I guess I just need to make you mad."

Keeley jerked her knee away. "You are so ... so ..."

"So wonderful? Majestic?" He lifted the cup till the straw was touching her bottom lip. "You want a sip?"

She pushed the cup away. "I was going to say infuriating."

"But it got you talking."

He didn't get it. That girl on the phone wasn't who she was, but who she wanted to be. How could she explain that to him without sounding crazy?

"Hey, want to get out of here?" he asked.

She wasn't sure that was such a great idea. She felt comfortable at Java Hut. "And go where?"

He jerked his head to the pier. "We can walk around. See what's happening."

She nodded. It was worth a shot. Then she remembered Nicky and their plans. "Actually, I'm supposed to meet my friend at the arcade after this."

"So you don't want to go, then?" he asked. She couldn't tell if he was disappointed.

"Um, well ... you could come with if you want. I'm supposed to meet her in half an hour."

"Sounds good to me. Better bring your A game. I dominate at air hockey."

They left the safety of Java Hut, and Keeley felt as awkward as before. She cleared her throat and tried to think of something to say. "So ... how was football camp?" she said as they walked toward the beach.

"Exhausting, but worth it. We got a new kid who's a great punter." He paused. "Wait. Are you a football fan? We never really discussed that."

"I kind of have to be since my brother plays."

"I didn't know he played." Then Talon gave a short laugh. "I love that I don't know. Everyone wants to talk football, but with you ..."

She completely understood. He saw her, not Zach's sister. "It's nice, isn't it? I love my brother, but I don't want to always be talking about the great Zach Brewer."

Talon stopped abruptly. "Brewer?"

"We're twins. Everyone says we look the same, except Zach got the dimples and I didn't. See?" She pointed to her cheek and grinned.

"Shit," he muttered. He glanced at her, his eyes widening as if seeing her for the first time, then looked away.

She bit the inside of her mouth. He looked angry. Did he know Zach? Had Zach done something to him? Worried, she reached out to touch him, but he flinched. Her hand dropped and she felt her heart do the same. "Are you okay?"

Jamming a hand in the front pocket of his jeans, he pulled out her phone and gave her an unreadable look. Grabbing his phone from her hand, he said, "It was nice meeting you, Keeley." Then he placed her phone in her open palm and strode away.

"Where are you going?" she called out. She thought he was going to turn back, but he didn't. Soon, he was no more than a speck in the distance.

Confused and hurt, Keeley called Nicky from her own phone.

"He just left? With no explanation?" asked Nicky.

"Like he couldn't get away fast enough." Keeley ignored the people milling around. Java Hut was starting to get busy, but she stayed where she was. Maybe a small part of her was hoping Talon would come back.

"It was probably for the best. Did you really want to hang out with someone like that?"

"Someone like what?"

"You know, the overconfident guy who has testosterone to spare."

"He's not like that." Or he was, but it wasn't all he was.

"Is he hot?"

Silence.

"My point exactly. His looks are blinding you."

It wasn't just his looks that caught her attention. There was something else that called to her — a complexity she hadn't noticed at first. She thought of his willingness to help her. She thought of his issues with his father. Yeah. There was depth. "He ... surprises me." Keeley tucked a piece of hair behind her ear. "Pretty stupid, huh?"

"Not stupid if that's the way you feel." Nicky cleared her throat. "Maybe you should call him."

"And say what?"

"'Hey, Talon, want to be friends?'"

She thought they *were* friends. What a joke.

Chapter 9

iDon't Understand

●●●

Keeley sighed a little as she pulled into the school parking lot. First day of senior year and her last first day at Edgewood High. She wanted to savor the experience, but her heart wasn't in it.

Zach glanced over. "Nervous?"

"Didn't sleep much last night." She'd been rereading her texts with Talon. Maybe she'd imagined their connection.

"That's what happens when you procrastinate. You did finish the stats homework, right?"

She didn't correct him. Better he thought it was about homework than a guy. "Everything's done." Thanks to Talon. She couldn't have finished without him.

Zach gently tugged a lock of her hair. "You sure you're okay? You look sad."

His concern touched her. "Yeah, I'm fine. And hey, good news. You can take the car. Nicky'll take me home."

"You sure? Cort said he would drive me after practice."

"I want to go with Nicky. Haven't seen her much."

"I noticed. What's up with that? You're usually joined at the hip."

She didn't want to explain. Not to him. "You wouldn't get it."

"Try me. Back in the day, we were the ones joined at the hip."

The memory made her smile. "We even shared the same blankie. Mom had to cut it in two when we were old enough for our own beds. But I would always sneak in when I got scared."

"And you hogged the covers. Man, you used to come to me for everything."

"Yeah, I did," she said fondly. Then she playfully nudged his arm. "But then you got into football and became too cool."

His grin faded. "We better go. Don't want to be late."

They got out and she handed him the keys. She was halfway across the parking lot when he called her name and said, "Catch."

With her lack of hand-eye coordination, she completely missed, but luckily it landed by her feet. It was Zach's Batman eraser. The one he'd given her the first day of kindergarten. It was a nub now, barely enough to use. She hadn't realized he'd kept it.

"For luck," he told her. "This is our last year together. Let's make it the best, okay?"

She pushed her sadness to the side and gave Zach a firm nod. They'd make this the best year yet.

Keeley could feel the excitement in the air as groups gathered in the hallways and friends rushed to find one another. When she got to her locker, Nicky was already there. She was wearing a cute dress, but wore sneakers so they could match. Nicky pulled a paper out of her binder. "Brace yourself. We only have one class together."

"How do you know?"

Nicky waved the paper in front of her face. "I got your schedule when I picked up mine."

"Don't you have to show a photo ID?"

"I might have lied and said you had a bad case of the Cochin."

"Cochin?" Keeley frowned. "What is that?"

"I made it up. Told the administrator it's a rare type of virus that you can only get through chickens."

"So now people think I'm infected with some type of chicken flu?"

"You're welcome."

Keeley shoved a couple of notebooks into her locker. "And you're crazy. How did you even come up with that?"

"Well, you are too chicken to call Talon." Nicky folded her hands under her armpits and started flapping her arms like wings.

"I am not!"

"Did you call him?"

Keeley slammed her locker shut. "Forget about him."

"I'll take that as a no."

The phone went both ways. He could have called her. "What class do we have together?"

"Sixth period AP English with Mrs. Miller," Nicky told her.

Well, that was one class Keeley could look forward to. But first period? Statistics.

On her way to class, Keeley saw a boy trip and fall. His stack of books fell to the ground, making a loud sound. People snickered, but no one stopped to help. To Keeley's surprise, it was Gavin. Her brother's freshman buddy.

She picked up a book. AP economics. The same one she had. "Are these Zach's things?" she asked, handing it to him.

Gavin artfully arranged it on top of the others. "He wants me to store these till after lunch. Thanks for the help."

"Rough morning?"

He shrugged, refusing to meet her gaze. "It's okay."

"It gets better, you know."

"What does?"

"Getting ordered around by the senior football players. They're usually toughest at the beginning of the year." She remembered Zach's first year. He'd been worried, too, but they got through it together.

"How would you know?" asked Gavin.

"Who do you think helped Zach? One time during finals week, his mentor called in the middle of the night and wanted fast food. We rode our bikes all over town and finally found a twenty-four-hour burrito stand."

"My cousin told me what to expect when I signed up. I just thought he was exaggerating."

Keeley knew his misery like it was her own. She leaned in and whispered, "I'll let you in on a secret. The whole point of this is to force you to bond with your freshman teammates."

"I can bond without having to carry all of Zach's books. Your brother is bossy."

"That's no secret. He bosses me around even though I'm technically older." Gavin's gaze moved to something behind her. It was a poster of their high school's mascot crushing Crosswell's mascot. "Ah, the famous rivalry. You know about that, right?"

"I've heard it's intense, especially between the football teams."

"That's an understatement." It'd become worse since Zach joined the team. He seemed to encourage the rivalry.

The warning bell rang.

"Before you go." She wrote a couple numbers on a blank page in her notebook and tore it out. "My locker and combo. Use it. It's in the middle of campus. It'll be easier to store your stuff."

Gavin looked at her like she'd just given him a million dollars. "I'll make it up to you somehow. What do you want? Money? Food? My kidneys?"

"I'm good on all three, thanks. See you around." She texted Zach as soon as Gavin disappeared around a corner.

> Go easy on Gavin.

> Chill. Today he's only going to carry my books and get me lunch off campus.

> Off campus? Why?

Usually Zach got pizza or burritos from the school cafeteria.

Heard there's some nasty chicken virus going around. Not taking any chances on the school food.

Keeley burst out laughing. Nicky's fake flu just went viral.

The day passed in a blur of back-to-school paperwork and what-I-did-last-summer conversations. And in the building fear of what she was going to do when the year was over. By the time she got home, she was in a full-fledged panic. Naturally, that was when Talon called.

She resented the flurry of nerves hiding in her stomach. "What do you want?"

"Keeley." He sounded slightly off. "Guess what? I've been drinking!"

So he drunk-dialed her. He knew she dealt with her brother's drinking all the time, so he ... What? Thought she'd do the same with him? "Goodbye, Talon."

"No! Wait!" he cried out. "I wanted to ask something."

To forgive him, maybe? Not that she was sure she would.

"I need an honest opinion," he said, voice solemn. There was whispering in the background, and then he asked, "Boxers versus briefs. Which do you like better?"

Disgusted, she hung up. Her cell phone rang again approximately three seconds later and she answered against her better judgment. "What?" she asked. Her tone so frosty her phone could grow icicles.

"I'm sorry! I was just kiddin'! That's not what I wanted to ask you. Let's say I was really, really ... really drunk and I called you."

"You mean like right now?"

"Would you pick me up?"

The answer was easy. "No."

The playfulness in his voice was gone, hostility taking over. "Why not? You pick up your douchebag of a twin all the time."

"Don't bring my brother into this." At least Zach never left her.

"I asked around. Learned all about you. 'Cuz I—Oomph!" There was a loud noise, and then his voice cut off.

"Talon? Talon! Are you okay?"

In the background, Keeley heard a scraping noise and then Talon muttering under his breath. "Stupid chair. Wasn't there before."

"Where are you?"

"At a friend's house. I just walked to the backyard. I need to sit down." He paused. "What was I saying?"

"How amazing you think I am."

"You are, you know. Keeley Anne Brewer. Twin of the famous football star Zachary Brewer. Senior at Edgewood. Loves reading. But I don't get something. It doesn't make sense. How come no one knows you?"

"What are you talking about?"

"Your texts."

She sucked in a breath.

"No one gets it. They think you're ..." He paused. She could hear the harsh sound of his breathing. "Why are you so different on here? Is it me? Are you different with me?"

She'd wrestled with the same question. She knew she'd acted different in the texts. Why did Talon bring out this other side of her? More confident and flirty?

Well, she wasn't admitting anything to him. Not after the way he'd treated her. "Of course not," she told him. Then she asked what she'd been dying to know. "Why did you leave me at the Hut the other day? I thought everything was going great."

"Does it even matter? Not like we're going to see each other again."

"We could if we wanted to."

"We can't."

"Then why the hell did you call me?" He was yanking her around and it wasn't fair.

"I don't know! I just wanted to — Argh!" he cried out in frustration. There was a loud bang, like something had been kicked over.

"Talon?" The line between them felt fragile. "What did you want —"

"Just forget it." With that, he hung up.

Chapter 10

iNeed to Move On

• • •

"All right, pens down, everyone. Pass your papers forward," Mrs. Miller told them.

Keeley's was riddled with crossed-out words and arrows, but she felt good about what she wrote. Then she saw Zach's paper, since he was sitting behind her. It was neat and concise. How'd he do that? They were twins. Weren't they supposed to be alike? "You're giving me a complex," she whispered to him.

"I messed up in a couple parts." He always said that, and then he got an A. Zach leaned forward. "Hey, can I have the car today? I want to stay after practice and work on my throws."

"Didn't you stay late yesterday?" And the day before? Zach knew he shouldn't overwork his arm. He could get injured and then he wouldn't be able to play.

"I know what I'm doing," he argued.

She glanced at Nicky, who made a what-can-you-do gesture. "Fine. You can have the car." But when he got home, they were going to talk.

Mrs. Miller stood up from her desk. "You're seniors now and that means college applications are coming." A collective groan went up. "In the next couple of months, we'll be working on your admission essays. These essays are important. They can be the difference between getting accepted or rejected. Now, you can write about anything — your favorite TV show, a unique hobby, a personal story — anything that shows who you are. I even had a student write about why he hated broccoli."

Someone called out, "Did he get in?"

"He did. See, it's not about writing how much you love to study or bragging about your GPA. This is your chance to show what those test scores, grades and extracurricular activities can't. So, this weekend, I want you to get started." She held up a stack of papers. "Here's a list of prompts to help you if you're stuck. Be sure to pick one up on your way out."

It was a relief her grades wouldn't be the sole factor colleges used to make decisions. An essay could be Keeley's chance to prove she wasn't just ... average.

When the bell rang, Keeley turned to Nicky. "Can I get a ride home?"

Nicky became apologetic. "I kind of already made plans. I'm meeting that college guy I was telling you about."

Keeley tried to look happy, she really did, but thoughts of Talon and the pier made it hard. She replied as cheerfully as she could manage. "That's okay, I'll find someone else. Go. Have fun. Text me the details."

She hurried to the parking lot. There had to be someone who could drive her home. She spotted Randy waving goodbye to his friends as he got in his car. She glanced around. Didn't have much of a choice. Running over, she tapped on his window.

He lowered it. "Hey, Keels. What's up?"

She hated that he called her that. Everyone knew it was Zach's nickname for her. "I was wondering if you could give me a lift?"

"No problem." He unlocked the passenger door and moved his stuff to the backseat. "Kind of like old times," he commented when she got in.

It was. His car still had that lemony-fresh smell she loved. "How was your summer?"

"The usual. Explored this awesome little town up the coast." They talked for a while, then Randy suddenly asked, "Who's that guy you're seeing?"

That's right. Talon had talked to Randy. "We're not seeing each other," she replied curtly. He'd only been in her life a short while, but she was reminded of him everywhere. It was completely unfair of him to breeze into her life, disrupt it and then leave.

"Oh. You okay?"

"Yeah, I mean, we weren't …" Dating. They hadn't even said they liked each other.

Randy looked at her out of the corner of his eye. "I know how hard breakups can be. I'm here if you need to talk."

And this was the sweet guy she fell for. Now she felt bad for not giving him the Barnett ticket. It wasn't like Talon was using it. "So, uh, about that Barnett tour this weekend. I still have a ticket. Do you want to go?"

He shot her the grin that once made her heart pound. "My cousin actually got one for me. He lives up there and sweet-talked one of the girls. We should hang out, though. It'll be good to be with someone I know."

He wouldn't be as fun as Nicky or Talon, but it was better than being all by herself. "How are you getting to campus? I'm riding the train tomorrow."

"Actually, I'm driving there tonight to spend some time with my cousin. How about I pick you up at the station when you get there?"

She hesitated. Being picked up might feel like they were dating again and she didn't want that. It was a step backward, but how could she move forward with her life when she didn't know how? The unknown was scary. And deep down, she wasn't sure if she *would* move forward even if she could. Fear was a powerful emotion.

Randy stopped the car in front of her house. "So, is it a plan?"

It would be rude to turn him down now. "Sounds good. I'll see you then." Ignoring the gnawing feeling in the pit of her stomach, she shut the car door behind her and went inside. Maybe she should cancel the trip altogether. But what about Zach? She couldn't do that to him. He was looking forward to her going.

Keeley spent the rest of the afternoon washing clothes and downloading books to read on the train. She kept checking the clock, waiting for Zach to come home. She needed to talk to him about his extra practices.

He finally trudged in after dinner, looking tired but pleased with himself. Keeley waited till he showered before knocking on his door. "You have time to talk?" she asked.

He was at his desk. "Yeah, just thinking of ideas for that college essay in English class."

"You going to write about football?"

"That's what everyone expects me to write. Do you think it's too obvious, though?"

She looked at the football posters on his walls. It was Zach's passion. "You could make it more personal. Talk about how it's affected you or something like that." While he jotted the idea down, Keeley made herself comfy in his beanbag chair. "How was practice?"

Distracted, he mumbled, "Good."

"Zach," she said firmly. When she had his attention, she laid it out. "I'm worried. You're spending all this extra time training. What if you hurt yourself?"

A confident look. "I'm in great shape."

"For now. Do Mom and Dad know?"

"Not exactly," he admitted. "But I've been careful. I *need* this extra practice."

"You never have before. Why now? Make me understand."

"I'm worried," he said in a low voice.

"About what?" Edgewood won all their scrimmage games this year. The team had never looked better.

"God, this is so embarrassing," Zach moaned as he buried his head in his open hands. "I'm worried about not getting into Barnett, okay?"

The admission blew her away. Zach never worried, at least not like this. "You have a 4.0 GPA and your SAT scores are amazing. You'll get in."

"No, I mean for football. What if they recruit someone else?"

"There are other football colleges."

"I've been dreaming of playing for Barnett since I was ten." He glanced at the bookcase where all of his football trophies were lined up. "I know they're looking at JT."

"The Crosswell quarterback?" Zach hated him. She knew it was because JT was the first to give Zach any real competition. They'd been trying to best each other since freshman year.

"Crosswell won the state championship last year. I can't let that happen again. That's why I've been practicing so hard."

It was *just* a game, but she couldn't tell him that. Football was Zach's life. "Barnett's not going to make a decision based off one game. You've proven you're good."

"I need to prove that I'm the best. Or at least better than JT. The big Edgewood-Crosswell game is coming up and I absolutely have to beat him."

She understood his need to win, but not at the expense of hurting himself. Why couldn't he see that? Passion must blind a person. Maybe it was a good thing she wasn't passionate about anything. At least she could keep a clear head. "You need to tell Mom and Dad. Or at least your coach."

"I know my own body."

Keeley wasn't going to let it go. Not when his safety was involved. "Tell them, or I will."

"You're serious." A dumbfounded expression. "Okay, I'll tell them this weekend."

"And you're not going to pull pranks on Crosswell again, are you?" He almost got busted last year.

His chin jutted out. "They do stuff to us, too."

There was no point in arguing. He would do what he wanted to do. "One more thing. Can you give me a ride to the train station tomorrow?"

He perked up. "You're really going? I thought you'd flake at the last minute."

"I wanted to," she admitted. But visiting meant a great deal to her brother, and she could use the tour as a way to see what she liked or didn't like in colleges.

"I think you'll be surprised how much you like it. What time do you need to leave?"

"Six. Bright and early."

After leaving his room, Keeley snatched her clothes out of the dryer and dumped them on her bed. Was she supposed to dress up for this trip? Or were her normal clothes okay? Nicky would know.

Keeley grabbed her phone and called. "I don't know what to bring. Am I supposed to be fancy and businesslike or casual?"

"Bring a couple outfits. Some nice, like that one blouse you have, and some more casual."

Keeley rummaged through the pile and found the green blouse. "I'm going to bring your floral skirt, too. How did things go with the college guy?"

Nicky groaned. "I read his text all wrong. He invited everyone from the study group, not just me. I don't think he'll ever look at me in that way. At least I get to go to the spa with my mom this weekend."

"I wish you were coming to Barnett with me. Sure you don't want to change your plans?"

"Thanks, but getting pampered sounds really good right now. You think Talon will show up?"

No, she didn't. Not with the way that phone call ended. "I don't get why he bothered calling." He'd already decided they weren't going anywhere.

"He called to mess with your head. You need to forget about him, Keeley. Just move on."

Nicky was right. Keeley needed to move on. Talon was a stupid summer crush that was distracting her from what was important, and Barnett was the perfect opportunity to think about her future.

Chapter 11

iFeel Unsettled

•••

The next morning, Keeley slid into her seat on the train. She grabbed her e-reader, excited to start another book.

"Is this seat taken?"

Keeley whipped her head around and saw a squat, burly man standing in front of her. "Sorry," she said with an apologetic smile. She really didn't want to spend four hours sitting next to a complete stranger. The man nodded and moved on.

The train jolted forward and started its journey along the coastline. Keeley leaned back in her seat and turned to the first page.

Then her phone vibrated with a text. Her heart jumped when she saw who it was from.

Talon: Excited about Barnett?

She leaned her forehead against the window, a grin spreading across her face.

Is that smile for me?

Her head popped up.

How do you know I'm smiling?

Reflection in the window. Turn around.

All the air in her lungs whooshed out. Heart pounding with anticipation, Keeley slowly rose from her seat. She set her knee on the seat cushion and turned to look at the passenger behind her. "Talon," she breathed.

He was casually leaning in his seat with his arms crossed over his chest. Keeley couldn't help noticing how handsome he looked in his blue hoodie and dark jeans. His piercing eyes were trained on her. He cocked his head to the side and smiled.

"Fancy seeing you here, baby doll."

He was here. He was actually here. She opened her mouth, but the words stuck in her throat.

"I guess I've rendered you speechless." He stretched his body and leaned forward in his seat, resting his arms on his knees. "I seem to have that effect on a lot of girls. Must be my unforgettable charisma." He sounded like he had when they first texted — self-absorbed and self-obsessed.

She wasn't in the mood for this. She missed the other Talon. The one she'd thought of as the real Talon. "The only effect you have on me is to my gag reflex."

Was he smirking or smiling? "I've missed this. Life's been dull without you."

"So that's why you're here? Because I add spice to your life?"

"Someone thinks highly of herself."

"I don't know why I ever thought inviting you was a good idea." Keeley plopped back down in her seat.

"Because of my chiseled body and boyish good looks?" He was hanging over the seat next to her, his arms wrapped around the headrest.

"I've seen better," she responded tartly. It was messed up, but she missed the banter, too. Felt like it made her come alive somehow. Why was it different with him and only him?

"My charming personality and quick wit?"

"Take your seat, Talon."

"Can't I sit next to you?" he said, motioning to the jacket she had placed to keep people away.

"I'd rather sit next to a cactus."

"Did you think I'd forgotten you?" he asked. "Don't worry. Your number is on my top-ten list of girls to call."

Her jaw dropped.

"Okay, okay! Top five. But that's all I'm willing to concede."

Keeley grabbed her earbuds and plugged them into her phone. She'd rather have Randy than this version of Talon. And geez, wasn't that comparison fitting. Randy had two personalities — one with his friends, one with her — and apparently so did Talon.

"What are you doing?" he asked.

"Ignoring you." She turned up the volume to make it clear she didn't want to talk, but Talon had other plans. He snatched the phone away and disconnected the earbuds. "Hey!" she cried. She reached out to grab it, but he jammed her phone into the pocket of his jeans. "Give it back!"

"Not until you tell me what's wrong."

"What's wrong is that from the moment you stepped onto this train, you've been acting like an ass. I thought those texts and calls meant something. That we shared — You know what? Never mind. Just forget it." First he abandoned her at Java Hut, and now he was being rude. It proved she meant nothing to him.

"Keeley ... that wasn't ..." A frustrated sigh left his lips. "I didn't mean to be like that. You just ... you were dead silent when you saw me. I thought you'd changed your mind about wanting me here so I ... yeah." He pinched the bridge of his nose and shook his head. "Look, can we start over? That wasn't how I wanted this trip to start."

She looked down at her hands. "Me either."

"I'm sorry for being an ass. Can you forgive me?"

She moved her jacket off the seat. As he sat, she caught a whiff of his cologne — a mixture of wood and Old Spice. He smelled good. The dangerous kind of good that could get a girl in trouble.

"You still have my ticket, right? You better not have given it to Randy."

"It's my ticket, not yours. And no, I didn't give it to him. He already has a ticket. He's at Barnett right now." She hesitated. Then added, "He's meeting me at the station."

Talon scowled. "He's meeting *us* at the station. Why is he coming? I thought you guys were over."

Was that jealousy in his voice? "I didn't think you were going to show up and I didn't want to go on the tour alone."

"So are you guys together or what?"

Definitely jealousy. "I wouldn't be, you know," —*flirting*, she thought — "if I was with someone."

Talon leaned in so their shoulders brushed. His gaze latched on to hers. "And just so you know, I wouldn't be, you know, if I was with someone either."

Was he really saying what she thought he was saying? His eyes dropped to her lips, and darkened. He drew closer, but suddenly Keeley's stomach growled. Loudly.

"Hungry?" he said.

Keeley turned her head away, not wanting him to see her reddening cheeks. Her stomach rumbled again like she was starving.

Talon stood up and reached above, where the luggage racks were. He pulled down a duffel. "My mom packed me the usual peanut butter and jelly. That's all my dad and I allow her to make. She's a disaster in the kitchen. Last time she tried microwaving, she ended up breaking the thing."

As he continued searching in his bag, something yellow caught her attention. Keeley leaned forward to get a better look inside. "Are those Peeps?" She pulled his bag onto her lap to take a closer look. "How many did you bring?"

Talon squeezed his eyes shut, looking slightly embarrassed. "Just six or seven packs."

Six or seven? Was he crazy? "You know we're only staying for two days, right?"

He stuffed a whole Peep in his mouth. His expression softened as he chewed and swallowed. He picked up another one. "I told you they were the greatest invention ever."

That phone call in Nicky's bathroom seemed like a lifetime ago. "They are not. If you were stuck on a desert island —"

"Yes, I would absolutely bring Peeps. A truckload of them. You could leave them out so they attract bugs and then use the bugs as bait for fish. See? Delicious *and* useful. Your turn. What would you bring?"

"Um ... I'd bring that British dude on TV who survives in the wilderness."

Eyes narrowing. "You want to bring him for his looks."

"That's not the only reason, but yes, his hotness is a factor." What girl wouldn't want to be stuck on a desert island with a man built like a model?

"He's not *that* hot. And if you're basing it off looks, why am I not a choice? I would bring *you* to the island."

A flutter in her stomach. "Is that so?"

"Of course!" He winked. "Who else keeps my ego in check? Okay, if you could have any superpower, what would it be?"

That was easy. "Flying. But no capes. Those things are a hazard."

"Flying would be my top choice, too, but I think it'd be cool to be immortal. You could do all sorts of crazy things."

"Like what?"

"Like free-fall from an airplane or go running with bulls. What would you do if you were immortal?"

Four hours later, they were still talking.

"You're wrong. Frodo is the hero," Talon argued. "He carried the ring to Mordor. He's the one who saved Middle Earth."

"Yeah, but he couldn't have made it without Sam. He's the true hero. Frodo tried to leave Sam behind and Sam still helped."

"It was an act of sacrifice!"

Keeley recognized that tone. It was his I'm-right-to-the-bitter-end tone. "Another stalemate."

"The zombie-apocalypse thing wasn't a stalemate. I'm right. A sword would be the best weapon."

"Swords are heavy! It'd slow you down and then you'd get eaten."

"But it's a sword!"

The look on his face was adorable and she couldn't help but pat his cheek. "Fine. You can have the sword, but I get Sam."

She was amazed at how comfortable she was with him. Reaching up and touching his cheek. She never would have done that with anyone else. What was it about him that made her so forward? Maybe it was because he was forward, too. He found ways to touch her arm and hands and would always brush her hair off her face. Even when she was looking out the window, he'd leaned forward so his lips were by her ear. Any time he said something, his breath would tickle her neck. Every part of her was aware of him at all times. It was a bit unsettling.

Keeley was having so much fun she didn't realize when the train pulled into the station. She saw Randy immediately, his red-and-white striped shirt making him stand out in the crowd.

"Seriously?" Talon whispered from behind. He was so close she could feel his body heat. "He looks like he escaped from the pages of *Where's Waldo?* How long did you date this clown?"

Grabbing his hand, she gave it a quick squeeze. "I get the situation is weird, but please act civil. For me." He squeezed back, but didn't let her hand go. She didn't mind. His hand felt big. Strong. She felt safe with him.

When they reached Randy, she made quick introductions. "Do you mind giving Talon a ride, too?" She should have texted and asked him, but she'd been preoccupied.

Randy looked surprised, but took it in stride. "No problem. I'm parked on the street. You're the guy from Keeley's phone, right?"

Keeley braced herself when Talon gave Randy a long look, but then he blew out a breath and said, "That's me."

When Randy's back was turned, she shot him a smile. He'd done as she asked. That had to mean something, right?

Chapter 12

iLike Him

●●●

"And this statue was created to honor our founding fathers who chartered the school in 1852," the tour guide said. "If you'll notice there's a small —"

Keeley rolled her eyes. She'd rather be on that desert island than here.

"Are you as bored as I am?" Talon whispered.

"Tears will be pouring down my face any second," she whispered back.

"We have to get out of here!"

"We can't do that." They'd been given a three-page schedule as soon as they arrived. They were supposed to be on the tour for another forty-five minutes, then dinner. She could see why

Zach wanted to come to this school. Barnett had a certain sophistication he would like. It wasn't her, though. She wanted something less rigid. More creative and open to ideas.

"I don't know about you, but looking at statues all day isn't my idea of a good time."

"We're not here to have fun." They were supposed to be learning. Concentrating on colleges and the future.

"If you can't have fun at college, then where can you? Come on. Let's explore."

She'd love to ditch the tour and go away with him. It wasn't something she would normally consider, but with him, it was different. However, she couldn't leave Randy. She rose on her tiptoes. He was standing at the very front. He kept nodding as the tour guide pointed out another historical fact.

"Baby doll, if I have to hear one more anecdote about a founding father, I'll bash my head in."

Keeley felt the same way. Hell, she didn't owe Randy anything. Wasn't like they came together. "Let's slip away after this. It's too noticeable now."

She really shouldn't be there, she thought. She was wasting the school's time and her own. Stupid Zach. This was *his* dream school, not hers. He knew that, too, but did that stop him from pressuring her to come? No! He was always doing things like this, too. Going behind her back and then making her feel bad if she didn't go along with his plan. She should just say no from now on. This was her life, after all.

When the group began moving, Keeley and Talon shuffled to the back. The tour guide directed the group to a building to the far left. Talon inched toward the right, motioning for Keeley to follow. As the group veered away, Keeley kept her head down and hurried after Talon.

"Now what?" she wondered out loud. They were behind an old building at the edge of campus. Alone. She was happy to be away from the tour, but now she felt a little shy. On the train, there were other passengers. Here, it was just the two of them.

"What's the thing you've been looking forward to most here?"

Him.

But she didn't say that out loud. "I don't know. Honestly, I don't know much about this place. Zach wanted me to come, so I did." How pathetic did that sound? "What about you? Do you want to see anything in particular?"

"I'm in the same boat. I don't plan on applying to Barnett, but you wanted me to come, so I did. I've been curious about you since we switched phones."

Her face grew warm. "Really?"

Talon looped his arm around her waist. "I came here to get to know you better, Keeley."

His words made her giddy inside but she also had questions for him. "Then why did you act like we'd never see each other again when you drunk-dialed me? And why did you just leave like that at Java Hut?"

He pulled her till he was close enough to drop his head onto her shoulder. Softly, so only she could hear, he whispered, "I'm always making mistakes with you, aren't I?"

She tried to ignore their close proximity, but it was difficult when all she felt was him. "Can you please just tell me?"

He pulled away. "I want us to have fun on this trip. Can we save the other stuff for later? Please?"

It was the "please" that did her in. Yeah, she could wait. She wasn't going to have a chance like this again. This new Keeley was going to go for it. "What do you want to do, then?"

He gestured to the building. "What do you think is in here?"

Keeley remembered the campus map. "A lecture hall."

"Let's take a peek," Talon said, grabbing her hand.

Quietly, they stepped inside. The class was huge! It looked like a miniature stadium. There were at least two hundred people in it, all furiously typing notes as a woman lectured about amino acids. Was this how college was going to be? Keeley noticed one girl playing a game on her phone. That was so her.

Talon nudged her and mouthed, "Boring."

She agreed. They might as well have stayed with the tour.

As they tiptoed out, Talon commented, "Wow. That was intense."

"No kidding." Somehow, seeing that girl made Keeley feel better. Maybe not everyone at college would be ambitious and directed. Maybe some of them would still be drifting, like her.

Her phone pinged.

Randy: Where are you guys?

Oh, man. Keeley showed it to Talon. "I don't know what to tell him," she said.

"Just tell him we ditched."

"But we didn't invite him to come along. It seems rude."

Talon looked at her like he was seeing something new. "Since when are you anything but direct? Here. I'll tell him." Talon grabbed her phone.

> Left. Be back later.

"Problem solved." Talon turned her phone off, then did the same with his. "There. No distractions. Just us and college."

But now what? They had no direction.

Talon didn't seem to have the same dilemma. He grabbed her hand again and tugged her to a different building. "Let's take our own tour."

They spent the rest of the day exploring the campus. They had no idea where they were going or what they were doing, and it was *fabulous*. There was no pressure to act a certain way or say the right thing. She could just be ... herself. Well, the version of herself that seemed to pop up whenever Talon was around.

Thank God Talon came on this trip. She shuddered to think about being stuck with Randy the whole time. Randy had never been this accepting of her. It always felt like he wanted her to be something more. More of what, she didn't know. It made her self-conscious. Like she was lacking in some way. But Talon ... well, he seemed to accept her for who she was.

It was getting late, and Keeley and Talon were wandering around one of the dorms when a group of rowdy guys passed. They were handing out orange flyers. At first, it seemed random, but then Keeley realized they were being selective. They were only choosing really attractive people.

"Party tonight, man," a guy told Talon. He gave Talon a flyer and completely ignored her. "Lots of free booze. And the *girls*." He let out a low whistle. "Finest on campus."

Talon handed back the flyer. "I'm good."

"Come on! It's going to be epic. We have an ice luge." Again, he spoke directly to Talon. It was like she wasn't even there.

Talon motioned to Keeley, including her in the conversation. "We're here for a campus tour. We don't even go to Barnett."

"Even better! I'll show you the ropes. Give you a taste of the *real* college experience."

"That's okay." Talon looked at Keeley. "I'd only go if you go."

His consideration touched her. If Randy were here, he wouldn't have consulted her. Heck, he probably wouldn't have even included her in the conversation. "I'm not interested," she said.

Talon looked relieved. "Sorry, man. Thanks for the offer, though." He put a hand on Keeley's back and whispered, "Let's get out of here." They followed one of the hallways, but quickly got lost. Finally, someone pointed them to an exit, but when they got out, they realized they were on the opposite side of where they came in.

"I forgot how close the beach is," she said, staring across the street at a long strip of white sand and blue ocean. Several palm trees dotted the area, offering some shade. Not that they needed it. The sun was almost set. Only swirls of orange and pink were left in the sky.

"I have an idea. Come with me." They walked down a street

that ran parallel to the beach. Stopping at a supermarket, he led her inside and then told her to stay put. "I'll be right back."

He returned several minutes later with three large grocery bags and a mischievous smile. He held out his elbow in a silent invitation and Keeley twined her hands through, following his lead. She trusted him completely. There was nowhere else she would rather be.

They crossed the street to the beach and took off their shoes when they reached the sand. He guided her to a small fire pit that still had wood left over from the previous user. He pulled out matches, graham crackers and a chocolate bar. It was like it was meant to be.

"We're going to make s'mores?" she asked.

His blue eyes twinkled in the moonlight. "Correction. Peep s'mores."

"Isn't it the same thing?"

Talon put the back of his hand on her forehead. "Are you feeling okay? You're becoming delusional."

Keeley smiled. "You're an addict. How many hours can you go without eating one? Three? Four? Do your hands start to tremble when you don't get your next fix?"

"Just sit your ass down and prepare to be amazed," Talon ordered, striking the match. While the logs started to burn, he assembled the chocolate and graham crackers. "Uh-oh," Talon said after opening the pack of Peeps. "I forgot to get something to roast them on."

The stab of disappointment took her by surprise. She hadn't realized how much she wanted to be here, roasting Peeps with him, till now. Well, she wasn't going to let something so tiny stop her. She'd find something. Even if it took her all night.

"Hold on." She ran over to a tree where she remembered seeing some sticks. She found two long, thin ones perfect for roasting.

"You're my hero," he exclaimed. Her heart drummed in her chest. Did he have any idea the effect he had on her?

He gave her a Peep, but not before making her swear not to burn it. They roasted the Peeps, then slowly slid them onto the chocolate and graham crackers. The Peep softened into a mass of molten marshmallow, melting the chocolate. Suddenly, her mouth was watering.

"Okay," Keeley said after taking a large bite, "I have to admit these are really good." The sugar on the outside of the Peep had melted to make a caramelized crust, giving a little crunch to the gooey treat. She had one more before calling it quits.

She watched Talon pull a puffed Peep off a stick and stuff the whole thing in his mouth. It must have been too hot because he grimaced and sucked in air, trying to cool it. He looked absolutely ridiculous like that, his lips pursed out, panting for air.

She needed to know something ... "Why Peeps?"

"What do you mean?"

"Of all the things to like — why Peeps?"

"Because they're awesome. Why else?"

"No. This goes way past just liking them." His obsession was unnatural. Knowing he wasn't being direct, she said, "There's a story here. Spill."

He turned away from her, the fire creating deep shadows

across his face. "I think it's because my grandfather always bought them for me. When I was little, I was ... well, I was fat. And kids were mean about it. Gramps found me in the barn crying one time. I was so ashamed. I thought he was going to tell me to suck it up and stop being such a baby, but instead he opened a pack of Peeps. He didn't say one word the whole time. We just ate, and when we were done, he patted my head and said he was proud of me."

"Sounds like the two of you were really close," she murmured, hoping she was saying the right thing. She remembered when Nicky's dad died. It had felt like she was constantly walking on eggshells.

"We were. We spent a lot of time together. He would take me geocaching on the weekends." At her puzzled look, he explained, "It's kind of like treasure hunting. We would pretend we were pirates and spend the whole day exploring new places. Everyone in our family thought we were crazy, but it was fun. *He* was fun."

"Do you still geo-whatever-it's-called?"

"Geocaching. And no. I haven't been since he died. I guess I could do it here but it's not the same. It was our thing."

Keeley knocked her knees against his. "You weren't really fat, were you?"

"I was. I swear! My growth spurt didn't come till I was thirteen. Right about the time I moved here. You should have seen how awkward I was."

"Is that why you don't have any pictures of yourself on your phone?"

He avoided the question by saying, "You don't have any on yours either."

"That's because I just got it. Your Peep obsession makes a whole lot more sense now. I'm kind of jealous. I wish I had something I was passionate about."

"Oh, come on, there has to be something."

"Trust me, there's not. I have to write a college essay this weekend. I'm supposed to be telling them about myself, but I have nothing to say."

"Maybe that should be your essay. A blank page," he joked.

"I'm serious! This whole college thing has been freaking me out. My life's always been the same. I've had the same friends, done the same things, and now it's all ..." She used her hands to mime an explosion. "I'm scared it's going to change, and then what do I have left? Nothing." Zach and Nicky would change and grow and leave her behind.

"I'll tell you what you have left — you."

"But what if I'm not enough?"

Talon massaged Keeley's shoulders, working out the knots. "Enough for what?"

"I don't know. Life. Family. Friends. All of the above."

"You're basing everything off what other people think. What do *you* think?"

She bit her lip, then leaned into him, letting him take all her weight. "I don't know."

Talon smoothed her hair down and rested his head against hers. "Baby doll, from what I've seen, the you that you are right now is pretty great."

Talon pressed a soft kiss against her forehead. Then another at her temple. Her breathing grew unsteady when he nuzzled her cheek. He shifted closer, and she shivered despite the heat of his body. In perfect unison, almost as if they planned it, he dipped his head down while she angled upward. Their lips touched.

It was a moment of admission. Her feelings on full display. She felt scared, unsure, but he accepted what she had to give and returned it with just as much feeling. He pulled away first, his breathing as rough as hers. Her eyes traced the contours of his mouth. He had been a stranger, but now he was so much more. She felt like she knew him better than anyone else.

"I've wanted to do that for a while," he told her.

"Me too."

He kissed her again.

Chapter 13

iWant to Forget

...

"Next stop, Main Street. Main Street, next stop," an electronic voice announced over the train's intercom.

"Home, sweet home," Keeley declared. She glanced at Talon, who was still passed out in the seat next to her. "Talon. Wake up," she sang in his ear. She was surprisingly energetic even though she stayed up for hours playing video games with some of the girls in the dorm. If this was what college was like, she could get used to it.

"Go away," he mumbled.

"Talon," she said again, this time louder. When he still didn't move, she nudged his side with her elbow. "You sleep like the dead."

"If I was dead, would you leave me alone?"

"You have to get up or we'll miss our stop."

He gave a long stretch just as the train came to a halt. They grabbed their bags from the overhead compartment and stepped onto the platform. "Do you need a ride home?" he asked, digging into his backpack for his car keys.

"My brother is picking me up."

"Zach?" Talon asked. He looked wide-awake now.

"He should be here. I texted him what time the train arrived."

Suddenly Talon grabbed Keeley's shoulders with both hands, forcing her to look at him. "Keeley … I-I …" he faltered and rubbed a hand over his face. "Damn it. Okay, listen, I …" he trailed off, looking slightly uncomfortable.

"What's wrong with you? It's not like you're meeting my parents or anything."

"Keeley —"

Her eyes lit up as she saw her brother. She waved her hand in the air, trying to gain his attention. "Zach!" she shouted.

Zach gave her a chin nod and headed toward them.

"Keeley," Talon said urgently, shaking her shoulders. "Listen to me. I have to tell you something —"

"Hey, Keels," Zach greeted her, while approaching them.

Talon's eyes closed for a brief second, his face a mixture of resignation and dread.

"Talon, I want you to meet my brother, Zach. Zach, this is —"

"JT," Zach said, finishing her sentence. "What the hell are you doing with my sister?"

"JT?" All the blood drained out of her face. It had to be a

mistake. He couldn't be JT. He would have mentioned it during one of their talks.

Wouldn't he?

Doubt started to creep in.

"Baby doll," he whispered softly, the words barely audible.

"What the hell is going on here, Keels?" Zach demanded to know.

She ignored her twin, keeping her eyes locked with the boy standing before her. "You're JT?"

Talon's face contorted. "Keeley —"

"You're the varsity quarterback of Crosswell?" The look on his face said it all. She had trusted him. She had confessed to things not even her best friend knew.

"Keeley, wait. Let me explain." Talon reached out to grab her hands, but she stuffed them in her pockets. "What I told you yesterday about waiting till after the trip to explain everything. I —"

Zach swung his gaze to her. "You went to Barnett with him? How could you do that?"

Keeley didn't appreciate the criticism in his tone. She wasn't a child who needed scolding.

Talon stepped between them. "Back off, Brewer. This is between me and Keeley."

Zach's nostrils flared. "There is no you and Keeley."

"I wouldn't be too sure about that," Talon shot back.

Did he really think they could pick up where they left off, even though he lied to her?

"What is that supposed to mean, Harrington?" Zach growled.

"Exactly what you think it means," Talon countered, his expression turning smug.

Zach took a threatening step toward him. "You better not have laid a hand on her!"

Why were they talking as if she wasn't there?

Talon straightened his shoulders, drawing himself up to full height. "I only did what she wanted me to do," he taunted.

Not only had he lied about his identity, but now he was lying about their relationship. Making it seem like more than it really was — they'd only kissed — but also, somehow less than it really was, too. Keeley's self-control snapped. "Excuse me?" she interrupted, her voice low and calm, belying her fury.

Talon's face paled when he realized what he had implied. "That came out wrong. I didn't mean it like that. You know I didn't."

"I don't know what you meant, *JT*. And a piece of advice? Acting like a dick won't make yours any bigger." She'd had enough. "Let's go, Zach."

"Baby doll, listen to me."

That nickname. It hurt so badly she had to close her eyes.

"It's not what you think. I wasn't playing you. It was real. It IS real."

She needed to go before she broke down.

"So, you're just going to leave?" he called when she started walking. "I never took you for a quitter."

"And I never took you for a liar. Guess we both don't know each other as well as we thought."

She got into the car. Her brother sat in the driver's seat, his hands gripping the wheel. His face was a mixture of anger and betrayal. "Do you want to tell me what the hell that was about? Why were you with him? And how do you even know him?"

"I don't want to talk about it right now." She wanted to go home and forget the whole incident. Forget she ever met him.

"Are you dating him?" he persisted.

"Drop it, Zach."

"Well, are you? I think I have a right to know."

Couldn't he see she was at her breaking point? "I'm not dating him. Now, can you just shut up and drive?!"

"What's your problem?" Zach asked incredulously.

"My problem?" Keeley repeated in a low tone. "My problem is that I don't want to talk. My problem is that I just want to go home." Her voice cracked on the last word, surprising both of them.

There was an awkward silence as Zach fumbled around looking for his car keys. "Um …" he mumbled, refusing to look at her, "have you seen —"

"The keys are in the ignition," Keeley said in a wooden voice.

Sitting in the car, driving home … everything was exactly the same, and yet it felt different. Maybe she was the one who had changed. This whole time she'd been acting like the girl texting Talon was separate, but maybe that girl was a part of her real self, one she didn't show many people. And you know what? She *liked* that girl. She wanted *more* of that girl.

The realization made her wonder about Talon. Maybe Talon was doing the same thing, except in reverse. The guy she met today at the station — the guy who got into fights and said crude things — was his true self, and the guy he showed her over the phone and this weekend was just an act. A lie. But even if it was an act, there had to be some truth to it, right? Maybe that person was still a part of him. Just not the whole part. But if she considered him a liar, did that mean she was one, too?

When they got home, Keeley headed straight to her bedroom. Tucker tried following, but she kept him out. She wasn't in the mood. Not with Tucker. Not with her brother. Not with anyone.

Her cell phone rang. It was *his* ringtone. Before she even realized what she was doing, she was across the room, grabbing her phone. She couldn't tear her eyes away from the screen, his name flashing brightly like a neon light.

Talon was JT.

JT was Talon.

Keeley hit the red reject button, sending his call straight to voice mail. Did he make up that name? Why didn't he tell her the truth?

Zach poked his head in. Gave her a cautious smile. "Left your stuff in the car. I brought it up for you." He set it down, then hovered in the doorway.

"I'm not ready to talk about it," she told him. Zach didn't move. She started to grow angry. "Why can't you just leave me alone? This isn't about you! This is about me and my feelings!"

"Keeley —"

She didn't want to hear it. "Leave me alone!"

"I just wanted to see if you're okay."

"I'm not. I'm miserable and angry and confused. There. Does that make you happy?" He just stayed there. Staring at her. "What do you want, Zach?"

Without a word, he walked over and pulled her into his arms. The silent acceptance broke her. Collapsing against him, she let the tears fall.

Chapter 14

iDon't Want to Listen

• • •

Three days had passed since Keeley learned the truth about Talon, and his betrayal felt as painful and raw as it had the moment it happened. Keeley found that burying herself in a mountain of homework helped. She even reserved a study room at the local library. Funny that it took heartbreak to drive her to work hard. There was no clear goal in mind, but maybe this would give her a direction to aim for.

She was in the study room, preparing for her first math test, when Talon walked in. "What are you doing here?" Keeley asked. How did he even know she was at the library? Did he follow her? She wouldn't put anything past this guy. She had no desire to see him or talk to him.

"I thought we should talk face-to-face."

"I have nothing to say to you."

He dropped in the chair across from her. "Good. Because I don't want you to talk. I just want you to listen. And can you please calm down and not go all *Kill Bill* on me?" he said, looking at her hands.

Keeley was clutching her pen like she was going to stab him. "Get out."

"No."

"I'm not doing this with you." She didn't want to listen to excuse after excuse. "You lied to me."

"I never lied," he stated matter-of-factly.

"Come on." Did he really expect her to buy that?

"Technically, it was an omission of the truth. My full name is James Talon Harrington the Fourth. A mouthful, huh?" He gave a sheepish smile meant to charm.

"So what the hell do I call you? James? Talon? JT?" The Easter Bunny?

"Talon," he stated firmly. "You always call me Talon."

Always? "You know what? I don't have time for this. I have to get back to studying."

"Then study," he said, unconcerned.

Keeley stared at him.

He stared right back.

"Aren't you going to leave?" she asked.

Talon put his hands behind his head and stretched out. "I'm good right here."

"You can't stay!"

"You can't kick me out of the library. It's public property."

Keeley pointed to the sign on the door. "This room is for studying and you aren't studying. So you need to get out." She would get an adult involved if she had to.

He lifted a backpack she hadn't seen from under his legs. "Then it's a good thing I brought books."

"Talon," she sighed.

He grinned at her from across the table. "You said my name. I consider that progress."

He was persistent, she'd give him that. "I can't do this with you right now. I need time."

"How much time?"

"I don't know." She couldn't put a number on her feelings.

He stood up and walked to the door. "I'll call you Friday night. We can discuss everything then."

Whoa. Whoa. Whoa. Friday was two days away. "I'm not agreeing to that."

"How are we supposed to get past this if you won't talk to me?"

"What is there to talk about? You hurt me. The end. What did you think was going to happen?"

"I thought I'd explain and you'd forgive me."

Did he really think it would be that easy? "I deserve more than a ten-second acknowledgment that my feelings matter."

"I never said they didn't," he scoffed. "It's like you want me to grovel or something!"

She wasn't asking for that. She just wanted some consideration.

"Fine. Prepare for some groveling," he snapped, and slammed the door behind him.

As Keeley was getting ready for bed that night, her phone beeped with a text. It was a picture message from Talon. Her eyes widened when she saw what it was. There was a blue marshmallow Peep sitting on top of a pillow. Next to the Peep lay an index card with the words "Sweet Dreams" scrawled across it.

The Peep reminded her of the bonfire at the beach. She'd opened up to him that night. Told him things she hadn't even admitted to herself. And that kiss. She touched her lips. That kiss had been powerful. She glanced at the text again. This at least deserved a response.

> Good to know "groveling" doesn't diminish your self-confidence.

Just my reputation ... but you're worth it.

> Cheesy doesn't suit you.

You haven't even seen cheesy yet. I can cheese with the best of them. Goodnight, Keeley. Dream of me. 😊

On her way to school the next morning, she received another one. She had to keep a straight face because she was with Zach, but it was hard. The picture had a blue Peep sitting next to a tall cup of coffee. The index card read, "Do you come with coffee and cream? Because you're my suga'." Keeley left the car with a little bounce in her step.

The pictures kept coming all day, all of them with a blue Peep and an index card. She got a picture of a Peep next to a pencil broken in two. On the card Talon had written, "Life without you is like a broken pencil ... pointless."

During lunch, it was a picture of the blue Peep in the passenger seat of his truck. The message said, "Are you a parking ticket? Because you have 'fine' written all over you."

Her favorite was the picture of just the index card that came during fifth period. It said, "Sorry, got hungry." She laughed loudly at that one, earning herself a sharp reprimand from the teacher.

No doubt, he was wearing away at her resolve. She almost wanted to text him back.

Friday came quickly and the picture messages didn't stop. Corny line after corny line appeared with a blue Peep till Keeley started to wonder how he still had any lines left.

"I've never seen a guy be so persistent," Nicky whispered when Mrs. Miller turned her back.

"Me either," Keeley confided.

Keeley's phone vibrated again. With one eye on Mrs. Miller, she pulled it out of her pocket and into her lap. The picture message had a blue Peep and a pink Peep sitting next to each other on top of a chemistry book. With a black Sharpie, he had drawn a cell phone with a question mark next to it.

Before she could overanalyze it, she wrote:

I'm ready to talk.

She hastily put her phone away as Mrs. Miller stopped in front of her desk. "Keeley? A moment after class."

She was nervous as she approached. She shouldn't have used her phone in class. She knew better.

"Keeley, I want to talk about your essay."

Her essay? Then she remembered how quickly she wrote it, right after finding out about Talon. A lot of her emotions had leaked into the writing.

Mrs. Miller continued. "I was surprised by your topic. It was very bold. I don't see many essays about fearing the future."

"I can redo it." She'd written about what she knew. It was a stupid idea.

"No. I like it. It was honest and real. The whole purpose of the essay is to see you, and I did. I think the ending is what you need to work on. How is college going to help that fear? If you can connect the two, I think you'll have a solid essay."

Keeley was relieved, but also confused. How *was* college going to help her?

A funky odor hit her as she reached her locker. Pinching her nose, she dialed her locker combination and pulled. The door swung open and a large duffel bag toppled out. The smell of chemicals surrounded her, so strong her eyes teared up. Something was familiar about that bag. She pushed the bag with her foot till it was facing her. On the side, the initials ZAB were stitched into the fabric.

Zachary Andrew Brewer.

It didn't look like football gear or clothes. When she unzipped it, she saw a small can of blue paint, a paintbrush and a roll of plastic wrap inside. The paintbrush was wrapped in a plastic bag, still wet from being used.

This wasn't an art project, Keeley was willing to guess. This was part of a prank.

Gavin skidded to a halt beside her. Panic formed when he saw the bag in her hands.

"What is this?" she asked. When she'd allowed him to use her locker, she thought he would store books, not stuff like paint.

"U-uh ..." Gavin stammered, looking uneasy. "It-it's a bag?"

"I can see it's Zach's. What did he do? And don't lie to me. I know this isn't for school." She had a feeling she already knew the answer.

Gavin wet his lips nervously. "I can't say."

"Did you guys do something to Crosswell?"

"I can't say," he repeated.

Keeley bit back the rest of her questions. Gavin was just doing what he was told. He didn't dare defy the older players. If she wanted answers, she needed to go to the source. "Where's Zach?"

"Eating lunch by the bleachers."

She handed Gavin the bag. "You may want to get rid of this before people start asking questions." Slamming her locker shut, Keeley marched to the football field where the bleachers stood. The football players were at the very top looking extremely pleased with themselves. "I need to talk to you," she said, calling up to Zach.

He put his sandwich away and headed down. "What's up?"

"Something stinks and it's not just my locker. I saw the plastic wrap and blue paint. You did something to Talon, didn't you?"

He gave her a long, level look. "You finally want to talk about him, and this is what you say?"

Guilt rose to the surface. She knew how hard it was for Zach not to push, and she appreciated his consideration, but she didn't want to tell him about Talon. It was selfish, she knew that, but Zach would only complicate matters. "Is this why you pulled a prank on him? Because of what he did to me?"

"I don't know what he did because you won't tell me. All I know is what I heard at the train station and it didn't sound good."

Keeley sighed. There was no way around it. She was going to have to tell him the whole story. "It started that day at the fair. We accidentally ended up with each other's phones and we couldn't switch back till later because of football camp. We started texting and I got to know him." She gave a brief rundown of the rest. "I had no idea he was JT," Keeley said once she finished.

"How could you not know? You've seen him at my football games."

"In his football gear and helmet. I've never seen his face." And it wasn't like she was paying a lot of attention to the opposing side. Her focus was on Zach, and she didn't even bother watching the game when he was off the field.

"You don't want to get involved with him, Keeley."

Sometimes Zach's competitiveness blinded him. "Just because you're football rivals doesn't mean he's a bad guy."

"You don't know him."

"And you do?"

His tone was fierce. "Keels, I'm not joking."

"I can handle myself. Now what did you do to Talon?"

"His name is JT, not Talon. And why do you care?"

"I don't think you should be starting anything." Once Zach started something, he always finished. Even if it meant getting in trouble.

Zach ran a hand through his hair, looking exasperated. "Why are you taking his side?"

"I'm not." Pranks weren't going to solve anything.

"He's just using you, Keeley."

"Zach, I don't want to fight with you," she said in a calm voice, trying to placate him.

"Then stop being so damn naive and open your eyes!" yelled Zach. Conversation over. Without another glance, he headed back to his friends.

Keeley was stunned by his words. How stupid did her brother think she was?

Even worse, though, Nicky seemed to agree.

"He's being completely ridiculous," Keeley told her on the car ride home. "He thinks I'm taking sides just because I don't want him playing pranks on Talon."

Nicky eyed her, as if gauging her mood. "Well, no offense, but maybe he has a point. I know he's been sweet with the Peeps, but the guy lied to you. Hell, he practically called you easy and you're just letting him off."

"I'm not letting him off," Keeley insisted. She just remembered the way he held her.

"I hate to bring this up, but have you ever considered the possibility that he's talking to you to get back at Zach?"

"The thought crossed my mind," Keeley reluctantly admitted.

Talon could be using her to get information about her brother. Zach always complained that JT would use every advantage in his arsenal to win a game. He exploited other players' injuries and weaknesses without remorse. Zach said JT was a ruthless captain, with no sportsmanship or respect for the game.

It all came down to one question: Who exactly was James Talon Harrington the Fourth? Was he JT, who'd stop at nothing to win? Or Talon, who'd stop at nothing to get her back?

Chapter 15

iGet Answers

• • •

The question was on her mind for the rest of the day, even when she was playing fetch with Tucker. She picked up the slobbery toy and lobbed it across the field for the thirtieth time. Keeley nearly jumped out of her skin when her phone vibrated in the back pocket of her jeans. Talon.

"Hey, baby doll."

"I liked the pictures. The Peeps were adorable."

He chuckled. "Peeps always win people over. Are you busy right now?"

"I'm at the park with Tucker."

"Which park? I'll come meet you."

Ten minutes later, she watched as a truck pulled into the

parking lot, the black paint gleaming as if it had just been washed. He greeted her with a candid smile as Tucker, who'd never met him, ran up, tail wagging. Talon crouched down and petted him. "You're the lucky guy that gets to sleep in her bed." He picked up Tucker's ball and threw it into the open field.

"So ..." She was too nervous to look at him, so she looked at his truck instead. "Did my brother do something to your car?"

He shoved his hands in his pockets. "Woke up this morning to it plastic wrapped and painted blue."

So that's what the plastic wrap was for. She wondered how Zach managed to wrap it without getting caught. Probably had Cort and Gavin helping him. What if Talon thought she had something to do with the prank? "I didn't tell him to do it. I didn't even know that he did something till this afternoon."

"I know. The thing with Zach and I — it's more than just ..."

"Right. Football." How could she forget their ongoing rivalry?

He looked uncomfortable as he shifted his feet.

A long stretch of silence passed between them. She tried to think of something to say, but couldn't. Finally, she glanced at him, only to find him staring back.

"I hate that you look at me like that," he told her.

"Like what?"

"Like I'm a stranger."

"I can't help it. I don't know who you are anymore."

"I'm still me. So what if people call me JT instead of Talon?"

"Then why didn't you tell me you were JT in the first place?" Keeley asked.

Talon's lips formed a tight line.

"Yeah, that's what I thought."

"It's not like that!"

Keeley looked away. He'd kept his identity a secret on purpose.

"Do you remember that first night we talked? The night we swapped phones at the fair?"

Keeley nodded. "Some of it."

"Well, I remember every minute. I remember every word you said to me. You were brash and annoying as all hell."

She remembered it, too. It had all been an act. But she liked to think she was growing into that girl.

Talon went on. "I should have hated you, but I didn't. I remember thinking how different you were from other girls. I liked it. I liked arguing with you. I liked getting you riled up. You didn't play nice just because I was some football star. So when you asked me my name, I told you it was Talon. Which was true ... in a way."

"That's a load of crap."

"In my experience, girls have these ideas about who I'm supposed to be. You don't get what it feels like when girls realize you're not anything like their image of a football player. It's like who I am isn't good enough. So sure, I panicked. A girl caught my attention and I wanted to keep talking to her. On my own terms."

Keeley was silent so Talon continued.

"Is that so wrong?" he asked, his voice raw with emotion. "I can't apologize for not telling you I was JT. You wouldn't have talked to me if you knew."

It was possibly the sweetest non-apology she had ever received.

"I can apologize for what I implied to Zach." He paused and swallowed hard. "I'm sorry, Keeley, for saying those things. I never meant to hurt you."

"Then why did you?" she whispered.

"Because I'm an idiot." His blatant statement made the ends of Keeley's mouth curl up. "But I'm not sorry for this." He reached for her hand, while his voice dropped. "Not sorry for getting to know you, baby doll."

Her heart was pounding. "Did you know I was Zach's sister before Java Hut?"

"No," he told her.

"Are you using me to get to my brother?" she asked, voicing her deepest fear.

Talon's eyes widened. "What?"

"You heard me," Keeley said softly, her eyes never leaving his.

Keeley tried to ignore the tiny thrill of adrenaline that she felt at the touch of his hand. "I've known who you are for a while now. In that time, have I ever even asked you about him?"

"No," she admitted. She searched his face for any signs of guilt, but there was nothing.

"I like you, Keeley. I started liking you before I found out about Zach."

"I like you, too." Those feelings never went away.

Talon wrapped an arm around her shoulder, pulling her into his embrace. "If you're worried about Zach, we can keep it a secret."

Keeley pulled away from him. "I'm not sure I'm ready," she said.

His phone beeped and he glanced at it. A reminder. "I better get back. My dad thinks I'm out running errands." She sucked in a breath when Talon leaned down and brushed a quick kiss across her nose. "How about we take it slow? Let me take you on a date. Tomorrow night. Eight o'clock. Are you free?"

She was, but should she go? It was only one date, after all. "Eight. Tomorrow night."

He was about halfway to his car when he called out, "Oh, and Keeley? Wear comfortable shoes."

"Comfortable shoes?" Keeley wondered out loud. She looked over at Nicky, who was sprawled out on the floor. They'd been working on homework since Keeley came home from the park. "Where do you think he's taking me?"

"Somewhere you have to walk a lot."

"It's weird though, right? I was expecting a movie or dinner at a restaurant."

"At least he's taking you out on a real date. Guys nowadays just want to hang out."

Now that Keeley thought about it, she never did have an official date with Randy. They'd just started texting and then boom — they were boyfriend and girlfriend.

Nicky propped up on one elbow. "Do you think going on a date with him is a good idea, though? The way things are with Zach ... It's bound to get messy."

"I know." But she was tired of letting Zach's issues rule her life. She wanted to make her own choices. Find her own voice.

Maybe then, she could become the person she saw hidden away. "But I want to at least try and date him. See where it goes."

"If you're sure, you're sure." Nicky slapped her book shut. "I better go. Mom's expecting me in twenty."

"Can't you stay for dinner? My mom made your favorite potatoes."

"That sounds so good right about now, but I promised I'd be home when she got off work. Save me some, though."

When they walked downstairs, Keeley's mom came out of the kitchen. "I was thinking we could have a game night tomorrow. Are you free, Nicky?"

Tomorrow? But that was her date.

"I'll bake a pie," her mom promised.

Nicky shuffled her feet, looking uncomfortable.

Keeley was torn. Nicky loved family game night. Since it was just Nicky and her mom, she didn't get to do many things as a big family. But she didn't want to cancel with Talon. She'd never felt this way about a guy before. What the hell. Game night could be rescheduled. And Nicky would understand. "Mom ... I have plans tomorrow night."

"Are you girls going to the movies?"

"Um ... well, y-you see ..." she stammered, the words getting caught in her throat. She was sorely tempted to lie and say yes. It would be a hell of a lot easier than telling the truth.

"What is it, honey?" her mom prompted.

"I'm going out, but not with Nicky." The answer got her dad's attention, too.

"Who are you going with?" he asked. "Randy?"

"No. Someone else." Keeley felt her cheeks flush.

"A date?" her mother asked brightly. While her mother encouraged Keeley to date, wanting her to meet new people and get out of the house more, her dad was more cautious. It took him a while to trust people.

"I'm just going to go," Nicky interjected, pointing her thumbs to the door. She waved goodbye before Keeley could stop her.

"What's his name?" her dad asked.

"Talon." She hesitated, then added, "But most people know him as JT Harrington."

An uneasy look flashed in his eyes. "Crosswell's quarterback? Number seven?"

"That's him."

"Ah. Does Zach know?"

She looked down at her feet, stabbing her toes against the hardwood floor. "Not about the date."

"You're going to have to tell him."

Judging by his previous reactions, Zach wouldn't take it too well. "I don't want to tell him yet. Not until I know if it will turn into something." Keeley paused. "Can we just keep this between us for now?"

Her parents exchanged looks. Finally, her dad nodded. "That's fine, but we can't keep it a secret forever. One date is okay, though, I guess ..."

"What time is he picking you up? Do we get to meet him?" her mom asked.

The thought of her parents talking to Talon made her nervous. "Is that really necessary?"

Her mom smiled. "Afraid we're going to embarrass you?" Keeley flushed. "Would it help if we promised not to show baby pictures?"

"I'd be more worried about the stories," her dad piped in. "Honey, remember that one Halloween when she was six? She wanted to give everyone in her class a special treat, so she passed out candy she found in your purse."

"Dad," Keeley groaned.

"Special treat, indeed," her mom chuckled. "Imagine my surprise when I got a phone call from the teacher asking why my precious daughter thought it was a good idea to hand everyone a tampon."

"Can you please not tell anyone that? Ever?" Keeley asked.

Her mom just smiled.

That night, Keeley had a hard time falling asleep. Getting to her feet, she walked downstairs with Tucker. She turned the corner and was surprised to see the kitchen light on.

"Zach?" she croaked. He was seated at the small table in the breakfast nook. A partially eaten pie was in front of him as well as his phone. "What are you doing up?"

He put his fork down and nudged his phone to the side with his elbow. "I could ask you the same thing."

"Couldn't sleep." After their argument, she wasn't sure where they stood.

He pushed the pie in the middle of the table. "Sit."

She grabbed a fork and sat across from him. They shared the apple pie, taking turns like they did when they were younger.

"What's going on?" Zach finally asked.

It was the perfect opportunity to tell him about Talon, but she just couldn't do it. "Thinking about next year. I have no clue what I'm going to do. Or what I'm supposed to do." It was true, but not the whole truth. "What about you? Why are you up?"

If she hadn't been watching closely, she would have missed the covert look at his phone. She grabbed it before he could stop her.

"Give it back," he demanded. He tried snatching it out of her hands, but she was too quick.

It was a photograph of Zach and a black-haired girl sitting together on a bench at the beach. His arms were circled around her waist while her hands were clutched together in her lap. The girl's body was angled into him, her shoulder and head resting against his chest. His head was tipped back, his mouth open with laughter.

Keeley had never seen this girl before. "Who is that?"

"None of your business."

Zach's hair was shorter in the picture and his cheeks were slightly fuller. Keeley realized the photo must have been taken a while ago. She zoomed in on the girl's hand. Displayed on her middle finger was a silver and blue class ring. It looked exactly like the one Zach supposedly lost his freshman year.

"Missing, huh?" she asked.

"Like I said, none of your business." He plucked the phone from her hands. "I'm going to bed."

She knew she was keeping secrets from him, but it never crossed her mind that Zach was doing the same. What else hadn't he told her?

Chapter 16

iHave a Date

...

The doorbell rang. Keeley raced downstairs before her parents could answer. Luckily, Zach was out with his friends so she didn't have to worry about explaining. Her hands trembled slightly as she smoothed her hair and straightened her clothes. It'd taken her over an hour to pick out an outfit. Finally she settled on jeans, her favorite purple top and white high-tops. She'd even curled her hair and brushed on makeup.

Everything was going to be fine. Maybe if she said it enough, it would be true. With one last check of her clothes, she turned the handle and opened the door. Her mouth went dry when she saw him. In the porch light, his blond hair was almost gold.

"Hey, baby doll. You look gorgeous." He stepped inside and hugged her.

She felt bad for pulling away so quickly but she didn't want to linger. Her parents were close by. Then she heard footsteps. Too late.

"You must be JT," her mom said, giving him a warm smile. Talon straightened. "It's nice to finally meet you. In all these years, I don't think we've ever had the chance to meet. Usually we see you across the field."

"Talon, Mom," Keeley corrected.

"JT or Talon is fine, Mrs. Brewer. I know the multiple names are confusing." He flashed Keeley's mom a grin and it seemed to charm her.

She closed the door behind them, making Keeley tense. What if she started showing baby pictures or telling embarrassing stories?

"Come into the living room," her mom said. "Are you hungry? I just whipped up some cookies. Peanut butter with white chocolate chips. Keeley's favorite."

"They smell amazing," Talon told her.

"Would you like some milk with them? We have ice cream, too. Vanilla, chocolate, rocky road —"

"Mom, we have to go," Keeley interrupted. She was going to offer the whole fridge if they didn't leave soon. Quickly, she steered Talon out of the house and into the driveway.

"She seems nice," Talon commented.

"She is. But she would have stuffed you with food till you

couldn't move." She climbed into his truck. "So where are we going?" Curiosity was killing her.

"Remember I told you about geocaching with my gramps? Well, we're going to the state park to geocache."

"I thought you didn't do it anymore." He hadn't gone since his grandpa died four years ago.

"I haven't." He tossed her a grin. "Guess I needed the right partner."

Butterflies erupted in her stomach. Geocaching was special to him and yet he was taking her. It was hard to wrap her head around. "How does this work?"

"Think of it as an outdoor treasure hunt. You use a GPS system to find specific coordinates. At each location is a container. If you find it, you get to keep whatever's inside."

"But how are we going to find anything in the dark?"

He explained that they would use flashlights to find small reflectors. Each reflector would point in the direction of the next reflector. All they had to do was follow the trail and they would find the container.

When they got to the park, she could barely see the faint outline of trees and brush. She'd visited once for a school field trip, so she remembered it was a heavily forested area with hiking trails and streams running throughout. Talon reached in the backseat to grab flashlights and handed one to her.

"Let's make this a little more interesting," he said as they walked toward a large wooded area. He directed her to a dirt trail that twisted out of sight. "A game of truth or dare. The first person to spot a marker gets to ask the question."

He was certainly full of surprises. "Okay. Any limits?"

"Nope. If you've been dying to see what I have going on under this shirt, now's the time," he teased.

"Plan on losing?" she taunted.

"I've learned not to underestimate you."

She patted his arm. "Smart boy."

It took several minutes before she spotted a small orange reflector. It was attached to an old, gnarled tree that looked like it'd been through a few storms. The marker pointed them to the right, paralleling a small stream.

She shot him a grin. "Truth or dare?"

"Truth," he answered, surprising her. She would have pegged him as a "dare" type of guy.

"What's the deal with your names?" The question had been bothering her.

"There are four James Talons in my family. It gets confusing, so we have nicknames. My great-grandfather was James, my grandfather went by Junior and my father goes by Jimmy. The first time Gramps held me, he called me Talon. It stuck."

"Then why does everyone call you JT?"

"I took Gramps's death really hard. I hated being reminded of him. So when we moved here, I decided to go by something new." He pulled a branch away from their path and let her go first. "Figured it could be a fresh start. I like that you call me Talon, though. It feels ... right." His gaze met hers and the impact felt like a kick to the chest.

She was happy he wanted her to call him Talon, but she wondered if the names were his way of differentiating between his true self and the football persona. In many ways, she and Talon mirrored each other. They both had two different selves, but she was trying to let her true self out. Was Talon doing the same? Or was he trying to hide it?

They continued on, following the stream. Large redwood trees lined the pathway. They were so tall, they hovered over Keeley and Talon, blocking out the light of the moon. It felt like they were in their own secret world.

Talon pointed his flashlight to a thick bush with white flowers. An orange reflector was wedged between the roots. They followed the arrow and turned north toward the rocky hills. She noticed large boulders and rocks, some of them precariously stacked on top of each other. "Are you sure this is safe?"

He dropped an arm around her shoulders and drew her close. "I'll protect you," he promised with a sly smile.

"Is this your plan? Get me scared so you can cozy up?" she asked suspiciously even as she wound her arm around his waist.

"It's working, isn't it?" he replied smugly, tightening his grip on her. "And since I found the marker, it's my turn. Truth or dare, Keeley?"

"Truth." She wasn't brave enough for a dare.

"How come you're different on the phone? It's like when we first met, you weren't the same girl."

Keeley didn't want to tell him. What if he felt different after learning the truth? She pulled away. "I — uh ... well, I guess I feel more comfortable texting." She picked up the pace and walked ahead so she couldn't see his response.

"So you're like that with everyone?" He sounded disappointed.

"It's different with you. I still can't believe some of the stuff I said. I just ... I don't know. At first, you were so cocky, and you made me so mad that I didn't care what you thought. I just said whatever came to mind."

"I guess I was kind of a jerk." He ran to catch up to her. Then pulled her close again and leaned down to place a kiss on her temple. His mouth was so close that she could smell the distinct scent of sugar and marshmallow on his breath. All she had to do was lift her head a little and they would be kissing. She wet her lips and slowly —

"Look! There's another marker." He dropped his arm and hurried to the rock formation in front of them. "Come on," he called out, motioning for her to hurry.

He seemed more excited about finding this cache than kissing her. They trekked up another hill that gave way to a meadow dotted with moonlit flowers. They continued till Talon spotted the fourth marker off to their right. It was at the entrance of a large cave.

"Oh, no," she protested when she realized where the arrow was pointing. "I am not going in there. No way. No how. There could be mountain lions in that thing."

"There are no mountain lions in this area," he said, trying to mollify her.

"That anyone knows of!" She eyed the dark cave with trepidation. What else lived in caves? Bears? Cougars?

"Come on, I dare you."

"I haven't picked truth or dare yet!"

"Do I have to get you mad again?"

No. Part of the reason she came on this date was to make decisions for herself. She needed to do this without help. Closing her eyes, she pictured how she felt sending those texts to Talon. Strong. Empowered. She didn't overanalyze or worry like she did in real life. She just did it. And she could do the same thing here. If she proved to herself she could be that brave version, maybe she could figure out what she should do after senior year.

Thrusting her shoulders back, she opened her eyes and walked straight to the mouth of the cave. Talon slipped his hand into hers and they walked in.

She moved her flashlight around the cave. A flash of orange near the ground caught her attention. "Talon, I think I found it." Her fear of the cave was forgotten as her focus narrowed in on the arrow. There were five or six large rocks piled together right below the arrow. She moved them one by one till she found a brown box.

Keeley lifted the lid. Nestled inside was a silver cell phone charm.

"So you can remember how we met."

Speechless, she glanced up at him. He must have hiked up to the cave before the date. It was incredibly sweet and romantic. How lucky was she that someone like this was interested in her?

"You know, I never collected on two markers," Talon commented. The smell of woods and sugar enveloped her. "Truth or dare?" he challenged, his eyes fixated on her lips. Every cell in her body came alive as she realized what he was asking. When she didn't answer, he leaned forward and nuzzled her neck. "Truth or dare."

Her pulse raced as he slowly moved up her neck, his nose brushing against her skin. Unconsciously, she angled her head to the side to give him better access. A shiver ran down her spine as he kissed the delicate underside of her jaw. His lips were so warm and soft. She closed her eyes as he kissed her again, getting lost in the sensation of his mouth on her skin.

Her eyes fluttered open when he pulled back slightly. "Keeley?" he said, waiting for her answer to the unspoken question that lay between them.

She slid her hand up his chest and wrapped it around his neck. She could feel his pulse jumping at her touch. He wanted her just as much as she wanted him. As she drew his mouth down to hers, she whispered, "Dare."

A second later, his lips crashed into hers. It was a hard, demanding kiss — nothing soft or gentle about it. She gasped as he wound his arms around her waist and hauled her closer to him. Instantly she melted against his chest, reveling in the feeling of his hard body plastered against hers.

Pleasure shot through her as he said her name, and suddenly she couldn't get enough of him. She wanted more. She needed more. Without thought, she tangled her fingers in his hair and pulled, forcing his head forward and his mouth to open. A harsh moan reverberated in the air as her tongue touched his. This was what she craved.

As their tongues danced in a rhythm all their own, she lost sense of time and propriety. She was drowning and she had no desire to resurface. In that moment, there were just the two of them — Talon and Keeley.

And it was perfect.

Chapter 17

iMake a Mistake

• • •

Keeley was in a study room at the library with Talon. She'd been coming to the library more and more. Being there helped her focus. There wasn't a TV or Internet to distract her. Talon studied with her most days, right after football practice. And secretly, she kept suggesting the library because she knew Zach wouldn't be there.

Her phone vibrated. Nicky. Was that really the time? It'd gotten so late!

We still on for dinner @The Factory?

Definitely.

Good. I need this.

What's wrong?

I'll tell you at dinner. See you then.

"Talon, can you drive me to The Factory? I'm supposed to meet Nicky for dinner."

"No problem. Do I get to meet the infamous best friend?"

"I can't believe you two haven't met yet." Their paths never really crossed because they lived in two different worlds — Nicky at school and Talon at the library — but Keeley was ready for them to meet. The Factory was a town away, where they were unlikely to run into anyone they knew. And she hated to be apart from Talon, even for a little while. "You should come with."

He rubbed his jaw. "You sure?"

"Completely. I want you two to meet."

"Good, because I'm starving." He grabbed her hand and kissed the back of it.

They walked over to his truck and she hopped in. She looked in the backseat. Piles and piles of Peeps. It looked like the factory had exploded in his truck. She was pretty sure he was secretly the Easter Bunny in another life.

They were halfway to The Factory when he started to fidget. His thumbs tapped against the steering wheel and he said, "So, I have a question for you."

"You need a Peep, don't you? I recognize the signs. Nervous demeanor. Twitchy hands." He didn't even crack a smile.

He sent her another quick glance before asking, "What are you going to do about Friday?"

Her forehead creased. "Um ... Friday?"

He exhaled deeply, laughing a little. "I should be insulted that you don't remember, but I'm not." He pursed his lips together. "The big Edgewood-Crosswell game. You're going, right?"

Her good mood vanished as dread took hold.

"Have you told Zach about us yet?" he asked.

"Talon ..." she trailed off, feeling uneasy.

"I hate sneaking around. I want to be able to go out with you without wondering if Zach is going to be there."

That's what Keeley wanted, too. Except ... "It's complicated." Zach was so focused on winning this one game, and she didn't want to do anything to keep him from doing everything he dreamed of. "I'll tell him after the game, okay?"

Face softening, Talon squeezed her hand. "I know we can handle it."

She should have felt reassured but the hint of fear in his eyes made her worry. Was he not as confident about their relationship as he appeared?

They arrived at the restaurant, but Nicky wasn't there yet, so they grabbed a table by the door. Talon slid into the chair next to her, leaving Nicky the seat across. After ten minutes, Keeley texted her, but no response.

When another ten passed, Talon suggested, "Let's order so it'll be here when she comes."

Keeley agreed, opening a menu and sliding it between them so they could both look. She wanted to get what she and Nicky usually ordered — a platter of finger foods and a side of pasta — but Talon insisted on trying something different.

"Live a little," he teased after the waitress left.

"We never order seafood," she informed him, grabbing a napkin and laying it across her lap.

"That's crazy. We're right next to the ocean. What about hot sauce? Please tell me you like that."

"Nicky and I both like it. The spicier, the better."

Talon pulled her in for a kiss. "You had me worried for a second. First, you don't think Peeps are the greatest invention ever, and now this? It could have been a deal breaker."

"I think your priorities are screwed." She watched as he leaned back and spread out in his seat. "You take up a lot of space, you know that? You did the same thing when we met at Java Hut the first time."

"That's because I was trying to get you angry then."

"And now?"

"Now, I realize getting you talking is a mistake," he joked.

"Hey!" She started tickling him, trying to find a good spot.

"Kidding! I'm kidding," he howled, squirming away.

That's when Nicky finally walked in. "I'm so sorry! I stopped for gas and then my phone died ... Oh." Nicky's grin faded into a thin line. "I didn't know you were bringing him."

"I hope you don't mind," Keeley said, pulling away. "It's just that I wanted you guys to finally meet. Talon, meet my best friend, Nicky. And Nicky —"

Nicky cut her off. "I know who he is."

Keeley frowned. "Is everything okay?" Then she remembered

Nicky's text about wanting to talk. She'd been so excited about introducing the two, she'd completely forgotten.

"Peachy." Nicky sat down across from Keeley, her eyes glued to her phone. As she texted, she said, "Where're the menus? I'm starving. I haven't had anything since breakfast."

Keeley glanced at Talon, who raised an eyebrow, and then looked back at Nicky. "We already ordered. The food should be here soon."

Nicky made an indistinct noise and kept typing.

Keeley wasn't sure what to say or do. Nicky had a right to be upset. She should have asked first before bringing Talon, but this was just plain rude. "So, uh, I thought your phone died."

"It did. Thank God for portable battery chargers."

"Did you use the one I gave you for Christmas last year?"

"Yup," Nicky snapped.

An awkward silence followed. Talon cleared his throat, then draped an arm on the back of Keeley's chair. Keeley tilted her head, trying to catch Nicky's gaze, but Nicky wouldn't look up from her phone. Couldn't she try to be pleasant?

Talon squeezed her shoulder. At least one person was acknowledging her. She gave him a sad smile in response. Eyes flashing, he hauled her to his side and pressed his lips to her temple. She took a deep breath, drawing comfort from him.

The waitress placed several dishes in the middle of the table. Keeley pushed one of the dishes toward Nicky. She knew how grouchy Nicky could be when she was hungry. "Have some."

Nicky finally lowered her phone, but her voice grew tight. "This isn't our usual."

"Talon suggested it." She squeezed his leg under the table. "It's spicy. You'll love it."

"But we always get the same thing. It's tradition," Nicky insisted, looking hurt.

Keeley tried to appease her. "We can get our usual the next time. Just try this." She scooped some deep-fried shrimp onto Nicky's plate, then onto Talon's and her own.

"It's really good. One of my favorites," Talon added. He grabbed a small bowl of hot sauce and set it in front of Nicky. "You have to try it with this. You don't want to eat it without."

"Thanks, but I can choose my own condiments." Nicky pushed it away. She folded her arms and placed them on the table, then narrowed her eyes. "So, Talon. Apparently you're dating my best friend."

The confrontational tone set off his own. He dropped his arm from Keeley's chair and copied Nicky's pose. "Is that a problem?"

"I don't know. You planning on sticking around?"

"I'll be right here." It sounded more like a threat than a promise.

"Is that so?" Nicky's eyes darkened. She pushed her chair back and stood up. "I'm going to the bathroom," she muttered, stalking off.

Talon pursed his lips. "Well, that was fun."

Keeley rubbed her forehead. It never crossed her mind they wouldn't get along. "I better go talk to her."

"Do you want me to leave?"

No, she didn't, but she had to talk to Nicky. "Do you mind?"

His expression said, yes, he did mind but he was going to leave anyway. "Is she going to give you a ride home?"

"She will."

Talon didn't look convinced. "Text if you need me. I'll pick you up."

Wrapping her arms around his neck, she gave him a long hug. "Did I mention you're the best?"

"You make it easy." He kissed her forehead. "Call me later tonight? You can wax poetic about how amazing I am."

Chuckling, she shoved him away. "Go. I'll call."

She waited till he was out the door before entering the bathroom. Nicky was leaning over the counter, her head hung low. "Hey," said Keeley, feeling unsure of herself.

There was a long pause before Nicky lifted her head. "Hey."

"I'm sorry. I shouldn't have invited him."

"Tonight was supposed to be just the two of us," Nicky reminded coldly. "Just like it always is."

"I know. I just wanted you guys to meet and this seemed like the perfect opportunity." Couldn't Nicky cut her a little slack? She knew she'd made a mistake, but it wasn't like the two of them couldn't hang out another time. "Talon's really great. He's even been supportive about the whole Zach situation. I know you were on the fence about him. That's why I wanted to introduce you two. So you could see what I see."

"You're always busy now," Nicky confessed. "Ever since you met him, you've put me on the back burner."

"That's not true." She was always texting Nicky.

"We don't spend half as much time together as we used to. Whenever I call to hang out, you're with him or about to be with him. I feel like you don't make time for me anymore."

The accusation made Keeley defensive. And a little angry. "Now you know how I felt! All summer long, you didn't have time for me because of your college classes. I texted you constantly and you would answer about half of them." And she never complained, did she? She was happy for her friend.

"I was in class!" Nicky sputtered. "What did you expect me to do?"

"You weren't always in class. You went and did stuff with your study group."

"I couldn't invite you to that. You weren't a part of the group."

"You went to the arcade together! You couldn't have invited me then?"

"It was a spur-of-the-moment thing, Keeley. This is different. We had set plans and you invited your boyfriend along."

"I wanted you to meet him! Is that so wrong?"

"Yes! No. I don't know." Nicky took in a deep breath and exhaled. "I just ... I really wanted to talk to you tonight. Alone."

Keeley sighed, too. Okay, she had messed up. But she just wanted to make things better now. "I guess I got so caught up in Talon I didn't realize how much I was ignoring you."

That was all it took for Nicky to admit her own mistakes. "I guess I was the same way this summer. There was so much going on with the classes, and when those college kids wanted to hang out with me, I felt so special. I didn't want to share. But once class was over, they pretty much forgot about me, and then you were constantly with Talon and I ... I ..."

"You what?"

"I needed my friend."

All other emotions fled except concern. "What's wrong?"

"All my hard work at school might not even pay off," Nicky said. "My mom says money's real tight right now. Basically the only way we can afford college is if I get a full-ride scholarship."

"Oh, Nicky ..." She knew how much college meant to her.

"I know. It sucks so much. I've been working my butt off for nothing."

"That's not true. You have the grades. You can get a full ride."

"But probably not to the schools I want."

Keeley knew Nicky had it all mapped out: a good pre-med program and then right on to medical school. Her plan would crumble if she didn't build a strong foundation. Maybe that was even worse than having no plan at all. "Listen, why don't we go back to the table and you can vent all you want? We can order our usual."

"What about Talon?"

"He wanted to give us time together, so he left."

Nicky was skeptical. "Just like that?"

"Just like that. I know you don't like him, but can you try and get along? You're my best friend, my other half. It's important to me. Please?"

Nicky made a disgruntled noise. "Especially because your actual twin doesn't get along with him either."

She winced. So they had plenty of roadblocks. But they could get through them. She had faith. "I'll get on my knees and beg if I have to."

Nicky wound her arm through Keeley's and locked elbows. She pulled her to the door. "No need to beg. You can buy me a cupcake instead."

"Of course. One cupcake coming up."

"He was an ass. Better make it two."

Keeley bumped Nicky's shoulder in thanks.

Chapter 18

iBecome Nervous

• • •

Keeley wiped a bead of sweat off her forehead, then took another long gulp of water. Traipsing around the state park was much easier at night when the sun wasn't beating down. Her head whipped around when Talon slammed his phone on the picnic table. Lowering her water bottle, she asked, "You okay?" He'd been texting ever since they'd hiked back down the mountain after finding a cache hidden near one of the lakes.

"It's my dad again. He turns into this crazy person during football season. I hate it." Talon didn't speak of his dad that often. Keeley got the feeling they fought a lot. "He couldn't care less what I do in the off-season, but football time rolls around and suddenly he's dictating my every move."

"Why does he care about football so much?"

"I don't know. I think it's some sort of status thing. Growing up on the farm, my dad didn't have a lot of money, but he played football and it opened a lot of doors for him. Got him a scholarship to college. I think he assumes it's the only way I'll succeed. Which is insulting. I'm not a stupid jock. My grades are high."

Keeley wondered if Talon even liked football or if he played because his dad wanted him to. "Are you going to play in college?"

"If I didn't, my dad would have a heart attack. Don't get me wrong, I love playing. I just wish he would let me do it without the constant criticism."

"Zach would trade places with you in a heartbeat. My family isn't big on football. We go to all his games, but we're not die-hard fans." Keeley knew the basics, but couldn't talk anything beyond, like strategy.

"My entire family is — all my uncles, aunts, cousins. One of my girl cousins, Linda, played in high school."

"That's badass." And incredibly brave. "I wish I had the guts to do something like that."

"You can. Although maybe not sports. I've seen you run," he teased.

"It's not even about sports. I don't think I can get out there and make a big statement like your cousin."

"Who said it has to be big? The only thing that counts is if it's important to you, or at least that's what my gramps told me." Talon's stomach let out a growl. "I'm hungry. Do you have time to grab dinner before I have to take you home?"

Keeley glanced at the clock on his phone. "I have time."

He grabbed the empty water bottles scattered on the table. "Let me throw these away and then we can go."

She picked up his car keys and phone. "I'll get the air-conditioning started."

As she unlocked the truck, his phone beeped. It did it again. Then again. Must be texts from his dad. She went to turn it to silent but more texts popped up on the screen, from two guys named Mitch and Finn.

Mitch: You'll never believe who we saw at the store. CLAIRE.

Whoever that was.

Finn: Completely ignored us. Don't know why you were so hung up on her.

Mitch: Think she moved back?

Finn: Who cares? An ex should stay an ex.

An ex? She hadn't realized Talon had an ex-girlfriend.

When Talon hopped in, he checked his phone. He typed something, then slipped it in his pocket. "Let's eat," he said, his expression unreadable.

Keeley didn't know why she was so bothered by Talon having an ex-girlfriend. Maybe it was because he'd never mentioned her, not even when she talked about Randy. And if Talon had an ex-girlfriend, it meant he could be comparing Keeley to her at all times. She did it with Randy. Thankfully, Talon always came out ahead, but what if she wasn't as lucky?

At dinner, she tried to work the ex-girlfriend into the conversation, but either a waiter would interrupt or Talon would start talking about something else. She was starting to think it was a conspiracy. They were walking to his car when she decided to stop being subtle.

Looking him straight in the eye, she asked, "Talon, have you ever had a girlfriend before?"

He stalled. "Besides you?"

"Besides me."

"Uh, yeah. Once. My freshman year."

When he didn't say anything else, she nudged his side. "Come on, I want more than that. You know about Randy."

The ends of his mouth turned down. "Her name's Claire. She was in my art history class and we were paired together for a project. We hit it off and started dating."

"And ...? What happened?"

He sucked in a breath and slowly let it out. "I don't like talking about it."

Even to her? She thought they could talk about anything.

It was quiet as they turned onto Keeley's street. Talon parked half a block away so Zach wouldn't catch them. When they got out of the truck, Keeley turned to Talon, intent on giving him a hug goodbye, but he stopped her. "Are you mad?"

She wasn't mad. More confused. And a little wary. What didn't he want to tell her? "Was the breakup bad or something?" That's the only reason she could think of.

"You could say that," he admitted rather reluctantly.

"You can tell me anything, you know. I won't judge you."

He sighed. "I thought everything was great between me and Claire, but ..." He shrugged and looked away. "One day I got a text from my buddy Mitch. It was a picture of her and this guy kissing at a party. We'd only been dating for a couple months. I felt like an idiot."

He'd been cheated on? Keeley couldn't imagine this happening, especially to a guy like Talon. Most people didn't see it, but he had a soft heart. "I'm so sorry."

"The worst part was the guy purposefully went after her to get to me."

What kind of guy would do something that low? "Why would he do that? Does he —"

A loud ringing interrupted her.

"Damn," Talon said, pulling out his phone. "It's my dad again. I have to take this." He held the phone up to his ear, a small grimace on his face. The volume was loud enough for her to overhear.

"Do you know what time it is? You were supposed to be home ten minutes ago."

Ten minutes ago? It was only eight o'clock.

"Dad —"

"The game is tomorrow. You should be home resting. Not out with your girlfriend."

Talon's shoulders were hunched over, his voice hushed but urgent. "I'm not doing anything illegal so stop treating me like I am."

"So you've said. And don't think for one second I've forgotten about you storming out of the house this afternoon while I was talking."

"That wasn't talking, that was lecturing. And I don't see what the big deal is."

"This is no time for girls, son. You can date all you want after the season is over, but right now, your mind needs to be on football. This is your future we're talking about."

Talon blew out a frustrated breath. He twisted his body, shifting away from Keeley. "Dad, I'll be home in twenty minutes. We can talk about it then." He ended the call and gave her a smile, but she could see the anger swirling beneath. "Dad at it again."

"I didn't know he wanted you to stop dating me. Why didn't you tell me?" What else had he left out of their conversations? She was starting to get a bad feeling about this.

He shrugged and looked away. "Didn't want to worry you."

"Talon," she whispered, emotion radiating from her voice. "I don't want to get you in trouble."

"You're not trouble. Trust me, I've been in trouble." He reached into his pocket. "I know we haven't been together that long but I want to give you something. Will you wear my class ring?"

He held out a square gold ring with a dark-green emerald embedded in the middle. "Crosswell High School" was printed around the gem in block letters. A football was etched on one side while his name, JT Harrington, was etched on the other.

He was giving her his class ring? All of a sudden, their relationship felt more serious than it ever had. This was an expensive piece of jewelry. Her parents had been furious with Zach when he'd lost his. Was he really comfortable letting her wear this?

He pulled at the collar of his shirt. "You don't have to if you don't want to. It's just an idea I had. Stupid, really."

"It's not stupid."

"Then why won't you wear it?"

"I don't know what this means," she answered truthfully.

Planting his feet on the ground, he leaned against his car. Then he pulled her to him, one hand on her lower back, the other holding the ring. "It can mean whatever you want it to mean."

"That doesn't help."

He gave a crooked grin. "I know we haven't been dating long —"

"Not even a full month." It felt longer, though. Maybe because their relationship began way before their first date.

"But knowing you're wearing it, especially at the game tomorrow, is important to me."

"Why?" She didn't understand. It wouldn't affect anything.

He shrugged. "Wearing it feels like you're supporting me somehow."

"Of course I'm supporting you." Why wouldn't she?

"What about Zach? Aren't you going to be cheering for him?"

She bit her bottom lip. She hadn't thought about the logistics. She'd been too caught up in Talon and the newness of their relationship. She couldn't openly cheer for Talon, not if she wanted to keep him a secret from Zach.

Feeling her tension, he rubbed her shoulder. "I get it. I do. That's why I want you to wear my class ring." He brought his hand between them and opened it. The ring lay on his palm.

She was still nervous, but she got why it mattered to him. And how could she not accept it when he was being so understanding about her brother? "I'll take it on one condition," she told him. "I give it back after the game."

"Deal."

She had the perfect place to put it. Reaching back, she unclasped the delicate chain around her neck and threaded it through the ring. It jingled as it collided with the silver charm.

Talon fingered the miniature cell phone. "I didn't know you wore this."

"Every day." The chain was long enough that she could hide it under her shirt. It felt like her own little secret from the rest of the world.

His lips parted in surprise and then spread into a large smile. Seeing him smile at her did something funny to her chest.

"What?" she asked. It wasn't as if she'd just declared her undying love.

Half expecting a flippant answer, she was surprised when he said, "Makes me happy, that's all."

It made her happy, too.

Chapter 19

iFeel Awful

•••

"I hate pep rallies," Nicky commented as she propped a foot on the bench in front of her. Today was game day and tension was mounting. Last year's defeat couldn't — wouldn't — happen again. The football players vowed it. A loud cheer went up in the school gymnasium as the cheerleaders entered. They took their places just as music started blasting. The whole school watched as they tumbled and danced to the beat.

"You hate pep rallies because you're jealous of the cheerleaders," Keeley replied.

"I don't see why I didn't make the team. I'm peppy and loud."

"You can't even complete a cartwheel."

Nicky wrinkled her nose. "The floor was slippery. They didn't give me a fair chance."

Yeah, right, Keeley thought. But being loyal, she said, "You would have been the best cheerleader out there."

They watched as a girl was hurled into the air, completing multiple flips before being caught in the arms of her teammates. Nicky sighed. "Fine. I could never have been a cheerleader, but I would have been the cutest one if I had any talent."

The music stopped and the cheerleaders left the floor as the football players made their entrance. One by one, the school principal introduced them.

"And finally, number six, Zachary Brewer!"

The school erupted into thunderous applause. Everyone loved Zach, even the teachers.

Keeley stood up and clapped, shouting her brother's name. He was scanning the stands, searching for her. When he spotted her, he touched his chest right over his heart and caught her eye. She did the same and winked. The ritual dated way back to when Zach first started playing football.

As the principal droned on about beating Crosswell, Keeley zoned out. Absently, she toyed with the necklace that held Talon's class ring and the cell phone charm.

"What do we have here?" Nicky asked. She lifted the ring and studied it. "Why didn't you tell me about this?"

"He just gave it to me last night. And I only have it for this game," she rushed to explain. Then she hesitated. "Plus, I ... well, I didn't know how you'd respond, especially after what happened at The Factory." She didn't want to hear any rude comments that could ruin the special moment she and Talon had shared last night.

Nicky drew her eyebrows together. "I hate that you feel like you can't talk to me. I won't lie — I'm still not a hundred percent sold on him, but I am trying."

"I know." Nicky had asked for a redo. It'd taken some convincing on her part, but finally Talon agreed. They were planning on coffee next week. "And I love you even more for that. After the rally, we can sit down at lunch and I'll tell you everything."

Suddenly, the principal announced, "We need a volunteer from each grade to participate in a game. Show your school spirit!" Cheerleaders searched the crowds, pulling people from the gym bleachers.

Amy, a senior cheerleader, approached them. "Come on, Keeley."

"No." She put her hands up. "Absolutely not. You are not getting me down there."

Amy grabbed an arm and pulled her up. "It'll be fun!"

"Define fun," she grumbled as she let herself be dragged across the gym floor.

When the four volunteers were gathered, the cheerleaders brought out a Twister mat, except instead of blue, green, yellow and red dots, there were mustard, ketchup, whipped cream and chocolate syrup dots. The person who lasted the longest won their class free ice cream. All around her, students were egging each other on, bragging how they were the ones who were going to win.

Suddenly Zach was next to her. "Don't worry, Keels, it won't be too bad."

"You did this," she accused, throwing her brother an evil glare.

"I'm just giving you a chance to show off your moves." He ignored her jab to the stomach and moved to the side so he could have a front-row seat.

Rolling up the ends of her jeans, she listened as the principal read off the first set of instructions. Hesitating, she watched as the other students stepped onto a dot of yellow mustard. Zach waved her forward, a toothy smile pasted on his face. With a grimace, she placed her right foot on the dot, mustard gushing between her toes. Gross.

"I'm going to kill you," she mouthed to Zach. For the next few minutes, she contorted her body over the messy mat, getting her feet and hands dirty with various condiments.

She could hear the whole senior class cheering her on. She would win for them. After all, this was the last Edgewood-Crosswell game they would be a part of.

"Left hand, chocolate sauce."

Balancing on her toes, she carefully lifted her arm and placed it on the closest dot. The movement caused Talon's ring to dislodge from under her shirt. Like a pendulum, it swung back and forth, Crosswell's green and gold colors clearly on display. Maybe no one would notice it in the mayhem.

That's when Keeley saw Zach's eyes on her again. And then his eyes on the ring. Cort, who was standing next to him, whispered something, but Zach didn't stir. Confused, Cort followed his line of sight. His mouth dropped when he saw it.

Knowing she had to explain, she moved toward them, completely forgetting where she was. Immediately, her hands slid from under her and she fell onto the disgusting mat. The whole school cheered, loving the action. Ignoring Amy, who held out a towel, she made a beeline for her brother. "Zach, I can explain."

"I think that thing around your neck says it all." Automatically, her hand grabbed the ring, protecting it.

Their eyes met. A lump formed in Keeley's throat when her brother broke their connection and looked away. She expected the anger—so hot it almost scalded her—but she hadn't anticipated the hurt.

"Are you really going out with him?" he asked quietly.

She sucked in her lips and bit, not wanting to answer.

"Are you?"

Slowly, she nodded.

"All right, everyone. Time to sit down," the principal said, urging the students back to their seats, even though they were covered in a soup of ketchup, mustard, whipped cream and chocolate sauce.

Out of the corner of her eye, Keeley saw Amy coming toward her, ready to escort her back. "Zach," she said urgently, before she lost the chance, "I didn't mean to hurt you. I was waiting to tell you after the game. I swear."

"I guess this is payback," he murmured quietly. "I took his girl, so he takes my sister."

Girl? What girl? Zach glanced at Talon's ring again, and suddenly Keeley put it all together. He'd had a ring once, too. But he lost it his freshman year. The same freshman year Talon was dating his girlfriend. "The girl in the photo. The one you gave your class ring to ... it's Claire. You're the one she cheated with."

He flinched.

"Everyone to your seats," the principal announced, looking directly at her. "Now."

Keeley staggered back to her best friend's side. "You don't look so good. Are you okay?" Nicky asked, handing Keeley a towel.

"I don't know." Keeley wiped down her arms and legs. "Zach found out I'm seeing Talon. And get this—Zach stole Talon's girlfriend our freshman year." She quickly explained what she knew. "I didn't even know Zach had been seeing anyone." How could she have been so out of the loop? She knew they'd drifted apart in high school, but this?

Nicky looked as shocked as Keeley felt. "That's not possible. Zach wouldn't do that."

Keeley couldn't believe it either. Her brother was many things, but he had honor. Or at least, she thought he did. And was what he said true? Was Talon using her to get back at her brother? She didn't think so, but adding Claire to the equation made her question.

She looked for Zach after the rally but he'd disappeared. All she could find was Cort.

"He doesn't want to talk to you," he announced, his body shielding her from the boys' locker room. Cort acted like Zach needed protecting from *her*. That cut.

"Please, Cort." She felt awful for keeping her relationship with Talon a secret. Zach must feel so betrayed. "I need to see him." To apologize. She could ask about Claire later, after he played.

"He wants to clear his head. Leave him alone for now."

"Will you at least wish him good luck for me? And tell him I'm rooting for him?"

He gave a sharp nod and walked away.

Keeley went to the girls' bathroom to wash her hands and splash some water on her face. By the time she got out, the gym had cleared so she stepped outside, hoping to find Nicky for lunch. Instead, she saw Gavin sneaking around the side of the building. What was he doing over here? Wasn't he supposed to be with the football players? A tall, hooded figure crept behind him. Wait ... she recognized that hoodie. *Talon?* What was he doing here? And why was he with Gavin?

She followed as they tiptoed past the gym to the far end of campus. They were huddled behind the weight room, whispering to each other. Coming up behind them, she asked, "What are you two doing?"

Talon whipped around. He had a paint can and a brush. Was he crazy? He had to get off campus before anyone spotted him. Especially Zach.

She pushed him into a corner, looking around to make sure no one saw. "Are you pulling a prank right now?"

"Baby doll —"

"Don't baby doll me. Are you nuts? Do you have any idea what kind of trouble you could get in?"

"It's a harmless prank," Talon explained, but Keeley wasn't having it.

"And you," — she turned on Gavin — "why are you involved in this?"

Gavin glanced helplessly at Talon. "He's ... uh, he's my cousin."

The revelation blindsided her. There was little resemblance between the two except for their blue eyes. "And you're letting him into our school?" She hated the pranking that went on between Crosswell and Edgewood, but she did feel some loyalty to her school. And her brother.

"Don't be mad at him. It's my fault. I guilted him into it," Talon confessed. "I wanted to get back at Zach for painting my truck blue."

That had been just a prank. Petty, yes, but harmless. But Talon sneaking onto school grounds? That was a different matter. "Can't you just let it go?"

"Everyone expects us to pull something."

That was his reasoning? Suddenly, Talon seemed very much like the teenager he was. But, Keeley didn't want to argue about it now. She had more important questions on her mind. "Talon, why didn't you tell me it was Zach that Claire cheated with?"

His mouth dropped a little. "How did you find out?"

"That doesn't matter." She turned to Gavin, who was eyeing them like they were in a soap opera. "I need to talk to Talon alone. Can you leave?" She knew she was being direct but she needed to be. If she was going to find out the truth, she had to become that girl on the phone who didn't overanalyze, but went straight to the point. She waited till Gavin was out of earshot. "Talon, why didn't you tell me it was Zach?"

Talon swallowed. Hard. "Because I know how bad it looks for me. What happened with Claire has nothing to do with us."

How did Claire and Zach's cheating look bad for him? If anything, wouldn't he come out better? "So you're not dating me to get back at him?"

"No! In fact, I wish you weren't his sister. That's why I left at Java Hut. I knew it would get complicated. I thought it'd be easier to put a stop to it then. But I couldn't. I couldn't get you out of my head."

A sharp whistle caught her attention. She turned and angled around Talon. Two boys she didn't recognize stood off to the side. The shorter of the two wore a dark-blue cap and a gray hoodie. She guessed he was the one who whistled because he kept tapping his watch impatiently. The other was his complete opposite. Twirling a set of car keys on his finger, he appeared almost bored with the whole situation.

"Wrap it up. We gotta go," the one in the cap said.

Talon looked at his watch and swore. "We'll talk more later. After the game. I'll text you." He leaned down to kiss her, but she turned and gave him her cheek. She didn't feel right about kissing him. Not while she was processing what happened and certainly not on campus where her brother was.

As Talon drew away, she saw his pained expression. She squeezed his hand. "We'll talk tonight. Promise."

Talon squeezed back, then the three boys hurried past the weight room and out of sight.

After school ended, Keeley fished out her books from the locker and went to the parking lot to wait for Nicky. The game didn't start till seven so they planned on hanging out at the pier before heading back to campus. She was almost at Nicky's car when she saw a gathering of students near the back of the lot. Interested, she veered toward the crowd. On her tiptoes, she strained to see what was so fascinating, but there were too many people.

Through the throng of people, she could see Cort's car. It was plastic wrapped and painted exactly like Talon's had been. But Talon had taken it one step further. He'd drawn a middle finger on the hood.

"Oh, crap," Keeley murmured.

The crowd hushed as her brother and his friends pushed their way through the masses. Everyone stared, waiting for his reaction. If they were expecting an outburst of anger, though, they were sorely mistaken. Instead, Zach's spine went ramrod straight. His expression frosted over, his face a mask of cold, hard ice. The only sign of emotion was in his eyes, and Keeley was the only one who knew what it meant. This was a declaration of war. Zach was out for blood and he would be gunning for one person on that field tonight — her boyfriend.

Chapter 20

iAm Torn

...

"The game hasn't even started yet. Calm down," Nicky said, putting a hand on Keeley's knee. "You keep twitching like that and people are going to think you're on something."

"I can't help it." She jiggled her other leg, expelling some of the energy building up inside her. Every minute that passed increased her anxiety. It didn't help that the football stands were jam-packed. She couldn't move without getting trampled.

She watched as people passed by, proudly wearing their school colors. And it wasn't just the students either—parents and teachers were outfitted in Edgewood's blue and white; hell, even the mayor was there. There was everything from T-shirts to bandanas to face paint. It looked like the whole town had shown up for this game, ready to cheer their hearts out.

Her eyes traveled to the opposite side. The Crosswell fans were packed into the visitor bleachers, every bit as enthusiastic, their side a sea of green and gold. This rivalry went back as far as anyone could remember.

At the far end of the field near the goalpost, Keeley could make out the Crosswell players. They were warming up — stretching and passing the ball. She looked for Talon's number, but his team was too far away.

"I don't see why you're so nervous. It's just a game," Nicky commented.

Normally, she'd agree, but not this time. "You saw Zach. He's itching for a fight." When Zach got angry, all reason flew out the window. If he were angry enough, he could get physical.

Nicky waved her hand at the field. "The refs would interfere before blood started flying."

"And that's supposed to make me feel better?" Keeley didn't want anyone to end up in the emergency room.

"Nothing will happen. They both play offense. When Zach's on the field, Talon will be on the bench and vice versa." Thank God for small favors. She couldn't imagine what would happen if one played on the defensive side. It would be a bloodbath.

"I'm still trying to wrap my head around the whole Claire connection. What are the chances that he'd be the person I switched phones with?"

"Chance or a perfectly orchestrated meeting? It's the perfect revenge — use Zach's twin to get back at him for what Zach did with Claire." Any goodwill Nicky might have felt for Talon had disappeared as soon as she found out about Claire.

"I'm not going to accuse Talon of something based on speculation."

"At least think about it," Nicky said. "It could be true — you have to admit that."

Keeley had to get out of there. Standing up, she said, "I'm going to the bathroom."

Doubt plagued her as she made her way through the crowd of people and into the bathroom. Did Talon have a master plan all along? Was he pulling the strings on her puppet, using her to hurt her brother?

She didn't feel played. His words and actions seemed genuine. And their chemistry — God, their chemistry — no one could fake that. Confused and frustrated, she let out a loud groan.

"Is everything okay in there?" a voice said from outside her stall. "I have some Tums if you need 'em, darlin'."

"U-um ... I-I'm good," Keeley managed to stammer out. Cue the awkward silence. The faucet turned on and Keeley prayed the lady would be quick. The game was minutes away from starting, and if she stayed any longer, she would miss the kickoff. As if to prove her point, her phone buzzed. An onslaught of messages popped up on the screen, first from Zach:

Where are you?! I don't see you anywhere in the stands.

178

You said you were going to be there. Was that another lie?

Then Nicky:

Did you fall in the toilet again?

Zach:

Are you on Harrington's side?! I can't believe you would do that to me.

Nicky again:

Should I call 911?

"Oh, for God's sake," she muttered. Zach wouldn't even talk to her, and now he was complaining? She knew he was upset, but he should know that if she said she was going to be there, she was going to be there.

What the heck is taking the lady so long? Keeley thought to herself. She was aware of how ridiculous she was, standing in a stall, waiting. What happened to the girl who fearlessly confronted Talon earlier? Why did that girl always fade into the background? She needed to keep her at the surface, but the only way she could do that was by making the conscious choice to do so. If she did that, maybe it would become second nature.

With a firm nod, she lifted the latch and walked out. The lady, who was no more than five feet tall, stood in front of the mirror. From the back, she looked like a high school student. She wore tight jeans, fringed cowboy boots and a Crosswell jersey. Masses of blonde curls were piled precariously on top of her head, looking like they could fall at any minute.

However, when she turned around, Keeley could tell she was older. Not that she was old in any sense. There was a maturity to her face, a knowing that only came with time. She'd seen the same look in her mother. She was absolutely stunning.

"Hi there, suga'," the lady said.

Something in her voice nagged at Keeley's memory. She wracked her brain, trying to figure out what it was.

"You doing okay?"

The lady's eyes danced as she spoke. That's when it hit her. Those eyes. That accent. This was Talon's mom, Darlene.

Was this really happening right now? She almost wanted to look around and see if there were hidden cameras. A sharp knock on the bathroom door saved her from having to respond.

"Darlene!" a deep voice called. "You look fine! Stop primping and come out. We're going to miss the kickoff!"

"Men," Talon's mom said, rolling her eyes at Keeley as if letting her in on a secret. Another impatient knock. "I better go before his blood pressure starts to rise. He hates missing one second of our son's game."

Keeley watched as she strolled out like a model with those high heel boots. She caught a quick glimpse of Talon's dad. He was an imposing man, tall, with a fierce scowl. Keeley waited a few minutes before scurrying to her seat and sat down just as the players took the field. The energy around her was electric. Everyone was amped. She could only imagine how Talon and Zach were feeling. "All right," she whispered as the whistle blew, "here we go."

The crowd hushed as the players crouched down, getting into position. She could hear Talon's voice as he yelled, "One. Two. Three. Hut!" The ball flew into his hands. He moved left and then feigned right as he searched for an open player.

She'd be the first to admit that football held no interest for her. There was too much grunting, tackling and huddling. But something about watching Talon play had her mesmerized.

For such a tall guy, he was surprisingly graceful. While Zach was pure power, Talon had finesse. He moved like a panther, zigzagging through the defense, his long legs giving him spurts of energy. He was fearless and nimble and commanding ... and all hers. She finally understood why girls pursued football players. Claiming one as your own was a powerful feeling.

Talon's arm went back and then his wrist snapped forward as he threw. While everyone's eyes followed the ball, hers remained glued to Talon. His body was tense as he watched, his focus one hundred percent on the hurtling ball. When his teammate captured it, marking the first down, Talon punched the air.

He might complain about his father and the intensity of the game, but underneath all that protest was a talent that couldn't be denied. He deserved every award he won, even if Zach claimed otherwise. She couldn't say who was a better player — Zach or Talon — but she knew it was close. Very close.

By halftime, Crosswell was down by seven points. They'd gotten an early lead, but Zach and his teammates made a couple of great plays to put Edgewood ahead on the scoreboard. So far, both teams were behaving. There'd been a couple of hard shoves, but nothing serious. For the first time, Keeley started to relax. Maybe they would make it out of this game unscathed. She pulled out her phone when it vibrated in her pocket.

I could really use a good luck charm, baby doll.

Good luck charm? Like what?

Do you want your ring back?

No. Something much better.

What's that?

A kiss.

She imagined herself running into his arms and kissing him in front of all these people. But that wasn't possible so she did the next-best thing. She puckered her lips and took a picture.

Now I'm ready to kick some ass. 😊

Her happiness faded. Zach was playing phenomenally well. His throws were right on point. He was leading the team to victory. Would she be partially at fault if they lost? Guilt forced her to text her brother.

> Playing great! And of course I'm sitting on your side … look for me during the second half.

As the teams came out of the locker room and took the field, she saw Zach. His eyes searched the bleachers till they found hers. Maybe things were going to be okay after all.

The second half began with the ball in Edgewood's possession. Zach was on the field with the rest of the offensive line. Everything was going fine until the ball flew out of bounds on Crosswell's side — right where Talon was sitting. Keeley's hands clenched together as she watched her brother jog over to get it.

"Uh-oh," Nicky muttered, straining her neck. "This is going to be bad."

"Someone stop him," she said to no one in particular, running her hands over her forehead and into her hair. "Okay, maybe this won't be so horrible." She watched as Zach leaned down, reaching for the ball. "So far, so good."

Suddenly, her brother stood back up without the ball. Damn. She spoke too soon. Her heart stopped as he slowly straightened, his shoulders squaring off. He pulled off his helmet just as Talon stood. Her fingers sank deeper into her hair. Her focus solely on the two boys advancing toward each other. Zach moved slightly to the right, blocking her view.

"Can you see what's happening?" she asked Nicky, who had a better view.

Nicky swore just as Keeley saw Zach's fist move. Horrified, she watched as it swung forward, connecting with Talon's jaw. For a split second, the crowd was deathly quiet. Talon moved, but not to tackle Zach to the ground like she thought he would. Instead, he walked away.

A referee walked out onto the field with a microphone. Over the loudspeaker, he announced, "Number six, Zachary Brewer, has been suspended from the rest of the game due to disorderly conduct."

Keeley sought out her brother, who was standing by the sidelines. He threw down his helmet and turned to the stands. Immediately, he found her. The fury in his eyes pinned her to her seat. Cort put a hand on his shoulder, but he brushed it away and kept on walking. She watched as he retreated off the field. His fist swung out and hit the chain-link fence that lined the walkway. The harsh sound of rattling metal reverberated in her ear.

The rest of the game was tense. With Zach gone, Edgewood started to fall apart. They made sloppy passes and poorly timed tackles. Crosswell fed off their mistakes, taking full advantage. With five minutes left, the score was tied.

Talon and his team were trying their best to move down the field, but Edgewood was holding the line. As the end of the game drew closer, Talon became desperate. In one great action-play, he faked the handoff to the running back and instead tucked the ball into his arm. Confused, Edgewood's defense followed the running back, who pretended to have the ball. Quickly, Talon looked down the field and saw one of his receivers open. A second later, the ball flew right into the player's open hands. Crosswell fans cheered as the boy sprinted down the field. He was as quick as lightning, dodging the defense while moving closer to the end zone. The crowd rose to their feet, their eyes transfixed on the field. He was at twenty yards, then ten, then five ... then ...

Crosswell erupted into cheers. Fans started pouring onto the field, running toward the winning team. Talon was hoisted onto someone's shoulders, his fists raised in the air. She was happy for Talon, she truly was, but a part of her hated that Zach lost. He worked hard for this game. He believed — rightly or wrongly — that his whole future depended on it.

"Are you going to congratulate your boy?" Nicky asked, motioning toward the field.

Her eyes shifted from the crowd of Crosswell fans to the Edgewood locker room. A lone figure exited, his shoulders slumped. She knew who needed her the most.

Chapter 21

iWant to Talk

• • •

"Zach," Keeley pleaded, knocking on his bedroom door, "talk to me." Her head fell against the door. Ten minutes she'd been standing in front of his room. She'd coaxed, ordered, yelled, even threatened, but no response. "Will you at least let me know if you're okay?"

More silence. "If the reason you can't talk is because some psycho is holding you hostage with a knife, then cough once." A faint sound came from the other side. She knocked harder.

"I'm fine, Keels. I don't need to talk." He sighed in exasperation. "I just want to be left alone."

"You know me better than that. I would never leave you in a time of crisis."

"You make it sound like I'm on the verge of a mental breakdown."

"Well, aren't you?" Whenever he lost a game, he would go out with his teammates and blow off steam by playing arcade games. He'd never holed himself up in his room before.

She slid down to the ground and leaned against the wall next to his room. "I know how much you wanted to win."

"Winning isn't everything."

She almost choked. This coming from a guy who still bragged to the family that he learned to walk before she did. "Then why are you here sulking instead of hanging out with your friends?"

"I just ..." Something thumped against the door. "I let my team down."

He let himself down, not the team. "You know you're not God, right? The fate of the football team does not rest solely in your hands. They had chances to win but they blew it."

"They voted me captain. I was supposed to lead them, not get into a fight and mess everything up."

"Yeah, you messed up, and you got punished for it. But it's over now. Stop beating yourself up and move on. Don't let this ruin the rest of the season. And keep your temper in check next time."

"I tried, but it was *him*."

"Did he say something to you?" She almost hoped he did because from where she was sitting, it looked like Zach punched him out of the blue. Hearing about the way he stole Claire, and now this ... she didn't like the person she was seeing.

"He told me you'd been texting him during halftime. That you sent him a picture ..." He paused. "A kiss."

"That's what set you off? A little extreme, don't you think?" She didn't even get why he was so upset with Talon. After all, it was Zach who went after Claire. So why the hostility after all this time?

And why was she sitting here thinking about these questions instead of just asking him? *Conscious choice,* she reminded herself. Every time had to be a conscious choice. Her fingers played with Talon's ring. "Why did you do it? Steal his girlfriend in the first place?"

At first, she thought he hadn't heard. She was about to repeat herself when the door swung open. Zach was sitting on the floor across from the doorway, leaning against the bed. His head was tilted back and his hands were resting on bent knees. He looked sad. Defeated.

"What exactly did he tell you about her?"

"That she was his girlfriend and you purposefully went after her to hurt him." His head shot up and she sent him a disapproving look. "It's bad enough that you guys have this stupid rivalry, but to use a girl like that?"

"Look, I'm not proud of what I did. But he's out for revenge and will use anything in his arsenal to do it. Even you. Wake up, Keeley. I thought you were better than this."

"Me? What about you? Punching someone over a stupid picture of a kiss? Targeting an innocent girl? This isn't like you. Not the Zach I know. And how come I'd never even seen that picture of you and Claire till the other night?" She'd never felt so far from him than she did right now. "What happened to us?"

Zach sighed. "Do you know what I wrote about for my college admission essay?"

He wanted to talk about college? Now? "What does that have to do with us?"

"I wrote about why I first joined football."

"Dad signed you up. We were six." That's why his jersey number was always six.

"And the reason I kept playing was because I needed something to do. When you became friends with Nicky, you didn't need me anymore. You stopped coming to me with all your problems. And I felt … alone. Football gave me friends. Something to do. And turns out, I was good at it."

She never knew he felt that way. "I didn't think you wanted to talk about Barbies and girl stuff. That's why I turned to Nicky." And eventually, it had become natural to confide in Nicky, rather than Zach. "I'm sorry if I was shutting you out. I didn't mean to."

"I know. But ever since then, there's been this wall between us. We talk about the day-to-day stuff but never anything more. I've wanted to come to you, especially when everything happened with Claire, but I didn't know how. Maybe that's why I've been pushing Barnett on you. I thought if we went to college together, it would give us a chance to start fresh. Gain some of the closeness back."

Keeley felt guilty for being oblivious. Her brother had always been the strong one. She'd assumed he never needed her. How wrong she was. "I like Barnett, but I'm not applying there. It doesn't fit me. But that doesn't mean we can't build back our relationship."

"How are we going to do that, miles apart?"

Conscious choice. That's what it always came back to. "We make an effort to turn to each other when we're having problems. I could have told you about swapping phones right away, but I didn't. Going forward, if something happens, I'll tell you. And you do the same. No more secrets."

His mouth lifted. "I like that." Suddenly, he winced, as if remembering something painful. "I should tell you something. It's about Talon and Claire. There's more to the story than what he's told you."

More? "What do you mean?"

"You need to ask him," he replied. "You deserve the whole truth."

"Why can't you tell me?"

"I ... I can't." Frustrated, he banged his foot against the door. "She asked me for one thing and that's never to tell anyone what happened. I'm sorry, but I won't go back on that promise. Not even for you."

She left his room confused. What was Zach talking about? The whole truth. What more could there be? She grabbed her cell phone and texted Talon.

You free?

Yeah. Just finished with the parentals. You at your house? I can swing by to pick you up.

See you then.

Keeley felt anxious as she waited for Talon. What "truth" was she going to hear?

She answered when he rang the doorbell. Before she could move, he lifted her in the air and spun.

"What was that for?" she asked when he put her down.

"Celebrating, baby doll," he explained with a wide grin that made her feel uneasy.

He opened the passenger door to his truck and helped her get in. Fully expecting him to close the door, she let out a startled gasp when his hands grabbed the back of her neck and pulled her in for a hard, quick kiss. Grinning, Talon pulled back and closed the door. He jogged around the back of the truck and hopped into the driver's seat. After pulling out of the driveway, he reached across the center console and grabbed her hand. "I have a surprise for you."

He was so happy. She hesitated to bring up a touchy subject, but reminded herself that Talon liked her true self. He even encouraged it. "Talon, I want to talk."

"We will," he reassured her, squeezing her hand. "But I want to show you something first."

Glancing down at their entwined fingers, she said softly, "We really need to talk, Talon."

"It can wait. I found this great —" He faltered as he caught a glimpse of her solemn expression. "What's going on?"

She hesitated before saying it. "Zach said I should ask you about Claire. Something about you not telling me the whole story."

"Let's not hash this out right now," he told her, a hint of desperation in his tone. "I have graham crackers and Peeps. We can go make s'mores."

"I want to know, Talon," she said firmly. There was something both Zach and Talon were keeping from her. It wasn't fair. "I need to know."

He appeared at war with himself as he bit his lower lip. Then a fierce look of determination swept over him. Yanking the wheel, he pulled his truck off the road and parked alongside a beach.

What the hell was he doing?

A pair of burning blue eyes stared back at her. "You want to know what happened? Fine. Let's talk."

Chapter 22

iLearn the Truth

He pushed open his door and marched to her side. His body was rigid as he held open her door and waited for her to get out. Silently, she followed him as he trudged through the sand and made his way to the shoreline. The moon highlighted the crashing waves and the stars glittered above. It would have been a romantic moment if the topic had been anything other than an ex-girlfriend.

He finally stopped when the waves of the rising tide lapped against his ankles. Looking out at the sea, he jammed his hands into his front pockets and hunched his shoulders. "I'm not sure how to tell you," he started. "I never wanted you to know, but in the back of my mind, I always worried it would come to this."

What was he so afraid of telling her? Some of her old doubts resurfaced.

"I was always getting in trouble for being too reckless. Gramps warned me that someday I would regret not taking the time to stop and think before acting." He shook his head slightly and gave a self-deprecating laugh. "Damn, was he ever right. There's not a day that goes by that I don't wish I had stopped to think after finding out about Claire and Zach."

She shivered and rubbed her arms, and the motion caught his attention. Without hesitation, he took off his button-down shirt and draped it over her shoulders.

"I was so enraged when I caught them," he continued. "I don't know what was worse, learning about her cheating or knowing the person she betrayed me for was Zach. The night I found out, I confronted her. I demanded to know why she would do such a thing. I thought everything was fine. We had a great relationship, so why would she turn to Zach? Why would she betray me?" The pain in his voice rose with each word. "Why wasn't I —" He broke off and pressed his lips together. "Why wasn't I ... enough?"

"Oh, Talon," she murmured. Of course he was enough.

"Don't feel sorry for me," he barked, wading farther into the water. "I don't deserve it."

"What was her explanation when you asked?"

His shoulders hunched even more. "She said I was too intense. She wasn't ready for that type of relationship, and Zach ..." He swallowed. "Zach made her laugh."

"That's still no excuse for what she did. If she felt it wasn't working out with you, she should have talked about it first, not gone behind your back," Keeley said loyally.

"We all make mistakes," said Talon.

"You're defending her?" she asked incredulously.

"I understand why she felt the way she did. When we were dating, I was still dealing with Gramps's death. I talked to her about how I was feeling and what I was going through. It wasn't pretty." He grimaced. "Combine all that with the pressure of football and ..." He shrugged. Then he kicked the incoming tide, sending a cascade of water back into the ocean. "Let's just say it was the perfect time for Zach to swoop in."

Regret laced his voice as he continued. "I made a mistake, Keeley. A very bad mistake. And I'm terrified that when I tell you, you're going to walk away and never look back."

"What did you do?"

She purposefully sidestepped his comment about walking away.

"After confronting her, I left with my friends," he replied. "We went over to Finn's house and started drinking. I was getting really worked up over it. I kept going on and on about how she betrayed me. After letting me vent, Finn piped up and said it's too bad she didn't understand how it felt to be betrayed."

He paused and ran a hand over his face. "I remember the exact moment when it hit me. I was holding my phone, looking at the picture of them kissing, and I thought of the other photos I had of her." The muscle in his jaw popped as he gritted his teeth. "Revealing photos."

She realized what he was saying. "You ...?"

His gaze dropped to the ground, but not before she saw the shame in his eyes. "I sent them to my friends."

Dismay quickly turned to horror. Those pictures must have traveled like wildfire. She could only imagine what Claire's life would have been like. Turning a vulnerable moment into something so vulgar. Being betrayed by the one person you thought was safe.

"See?!" he exploded, throwing his hands up. "This is why I didn't want you to know. I never wanted you to look at me like that" — he motioned to her face — "sick with revulsion."

"I don't see you the same way. How can I?" This was not the person she thought she knew. She understood being upset and hurt at being cheated on, but to purposefully humiliate someone? It was cruel.

"You don't think I regret it?" he cried. "When I woke up the next morning, I tried to take it all back, but by then, the damage was already done. Everyone had the pictures."

"Is that why she moved?"

He nodded. "About a month after the incident, her house went on sale. She moved an hour north of here. I tried to apologize, but she refused to talk to me." He closed his eyes briefly. "You have no idea how much I wish I had stopped to think before sending those photos."

"Probably not as much as she did," said Keeley. She regretted it the instant the worlds left her mouth. "I shouldn't have said that." But she was right.

Talon shoved his hands in his pocket. "It's fine. So now you know. That's the whole story. And that's why I never keep pictures on my phone anymore."

Her mind raced as she went over everything she learned. She knew he was sorry. It was evident in every word, every motion. But despite all that, how could she trust him? What else was he holding back? And what else was he capable of? Being a hothead and making a rash decision was one thing, but he had ruined someone's life. What if he ruined hers?

Carefully, she said, "It's a lot to take in."

For a few seconds, she contemplated falling into his arms and assuring him everything would be okay, but her conscience intervened. "What you did was awful, Talon. You ruined that girl's high school experience so much that she was forced to move." And what about beyond high school? Those pictures could follow her to college and jobs ... and, ugh, what if her kids saw them?

"I would never do something like that to you," he swore.

"You say that now ..." She wanted to believe him, but ... her whole life was ahead of her. What if something happened and he jeopardized that? She needed to trust the person she was with, not constantly be on alert.

He picked up her hand and placed it on his chest, holding it there with his own. His heart beat rapidly under her palm. "I've learned my lesson, Keeley. I've changed. I know you don't believe me. And that's completely understandable. But at least give me the opportunity to prove I'm not that guy anymore."

His blue eyes compelled her to listen — to believe. If this had happened a month ago, maybe even a week ago, she would have. But she was a different girl now. One that could speak her mind. She knew what she needed to do. Drawing a deep breath, she explained. "It's the fact that you were that guy in the first place that worries me. It's like finding out about your name all over again."

"Trust me," he whispered.

"You ask me to blindly trust you, but when will you trust me? When will you tell me the whole truth every time?"

A shadow crossed his face. "When I know you won't walk away from me."

"That's not a relationship, Talon. Keeping secrets only hurts what we've built."

"Can you honestly say if you knew everything upfront, you would have given me a chance?"

Hesitation lined her face.

"Exactly! Don't you see?" He clutched her shoulders. "I was giving us time to connect, to build our foundation so it could withstand the secrets."

"You're forgetting something, Talon." She narrowed her eyes and took a deep breath. She tried to stay brave. "You were never going to tell me, Talon. Never," she repeated. "If I hadn't pushed, you would have happily left me in the dark."

"Why would I want the girl I care about to know my darkest secret? The one that I'm most ashamed about?"

Fury threaded her voice. "You tell me because it's the right thing to do. You tell me because we're equals. You have no right to decide what is right for this relationship and what is wrong." Her

198

brown eyes grew animated. "I'm in this, too. And I should have a choice."

"I did what I thought was best," he managed to say. "I made mistakes. I see that now, and as much as I would like to, I can't change the past."

"And what about the future? How do I know you won't do the same thing next time?"

"Oh, so there's a chance we have a relationship now?"

His sarcastic tone broke something in her. She scrambled to repair it, but it was too late. Tears welled in her eyes and slowly coursed down her face.

Talon rested his forehead against hers, gently wiping away the tears with his thumb. "I'm sorry, baby doll. So sorry," he whispered. "Please don't cry." His lips followed his thumb, pressing soft kisses against her cheek.

"I'm just so confused," she said. "Sometimes it feels as if I'm dating two different guys."

"I'm just me," he replied.

She wiped away the last of her tears and raised her head. "But you're not. Sometimes you can be Talon and other times you can be JT. When you're Talon, you're sweet and funny. But every so often, I catch a glimpse of JT. And I don't know how to reconcile the two." She thought JT was an act, and Talon was his true self, but what if that wasn't the case? "I don't trust JT."

His nostrils flared. "So what? That's it? You decide you don't like one aspect of me, so you quit? You're not even going to try?"

Her eyes burned as she looked away and quietly whispered, "I don't know if I want to."

Her admission hung in the air. All she could hear was the sound of his breathing.

"If you tell me right now there's no chance of us being together, then I'll walk away. I won't bother you again. But if you feel there's even the slightest chance of us working out, then I'll fight with everything I have to prove you can trust me."

With college and everything around her changing, she needed to feel safe in a relationship. Talon was no longer safe. "I'm sorry."

Keeley saw the pain slash through his face as his eyes closed. When he opened them again, he stepped away from her, his voice flat. "Let's get you home," he said.

The drive back lasted a thousand years. She would have felt better if he'd shown her some type of emotion, but she couldn't read him at all. It was as if a protective shell encased his feelings.

By the time he pulled into her driveway, she was anxious to get out. She had the door halfway open before he even put the truck in park.

"Wait," he said. "You have my ..."

She was still wearing his long-sleeved shirt. "Oh. You probably want that back, huh?" she asked. She slipped out of the soft fabric and handed it back to him.

"Thanks, but I actually meant my ring."

Her fingers fumbled with the clasp. Her heart stopped as she turned around to hand it to him, an emblem of what they'd lost. "Do you want the charm, too?"

"No," he whispered. "That was a present."

She gave him a sad smile and climbed out of the truck. As he drove off, she raised a hand and whispered, "Bye, Talon."

Chapter 23

iDon't Want to Be Alone

•••

Edgewood's Homecoming dance was fast approaching. The student body was abuzz as they gossiped about who was going with whom and what they were going to wear. For the most part, Keeley tuned them out, but every now and then, a stray comment would make its way to her. In those few moments, she allowed herself to imagine what it would be like to go to Homecoming with Talon. Which she would never be doing now.

When the lunch bell rang, she found Nicky at one of the cafeteria tables. "I am so sick of hearing about Homecoming," Keeley said. "I can't wait for our girls-only weekend." They planned to spend the whole weekend together. They were going to go bowling and to the movies and sleep over and pamper themselves.

A hesitant look. "About that ..."

Keeley felt dread creeping in. *Don't let it be what I think,* she thought. She didn't want to spend Homecoming weekend alone, this year of all years.

"Do you remember Ben, the cross-country runner I had a crush on? Well, he stopped me after English and asked me to the dance."

Keeley's stomach dropped. "Are you going?"

"I know we have plans and everything but ..." She silently pleaded for Keeley to understand. "It's senior year. It's our last Homecoming. I really want to go."

Keeley understood. She felt the same way. She had been looking forward to going with Talon even if he was her school's archenemy. She imagined walking into the dance with him on her arm. They would create a huge uproar.

"He has a friend who doesn't have a date yet. We could double," Nicky suggested in a hopeful tone. "It'd be fun! We could go dress shopping together, do our hair and makeup. And Ben and his group are even renting a limo. They'd pay for everything."

It would be fun to get ready together, but the rest of it? ... No. She couldn't imagine going to that dance with anyone but Talon. "Thanks, but I don't think I can. Besides, I wouldn't be a very fun date." She'd been feeling empty inside. Like a piece was missing from her life.

Nicky stood up. "I don't want you sitting at home moping. I'll just tell Ben no."

She grabbed Nicky's arm and forced her to sit. "Don't do that. Go to the dance with him."

"Are you sure?"

The eagerness in Nicky's eyes was proof she'd made the right decision. "I'll be fine. Probably binge-watch another show on Netflix."

She picked at her food, not really hungry. The worst part of the breakup was when she forgot they weren't together anymore. Like those moments when, waking up, she'd automatically reach for her phone, expecting a text from him, and then she'd remember what had happened. It was like breaking up all over again. "I know I'm the one who broke up with him, but I miss him. A lot."

"You made the right choice. You can't be with someone like that."

"Doesn't stop me from missing him. When I go to bed, I find myself reading our texts." She could see the progression of their relationship. How they opened up and then grew to trust each other.

"Delete those messages. Hell, delete his number. Make a clean break so you can get over him faster."

Nicky made it sound so easy but it wasn't. Keeley wasn't ready to let go yet. She liked the change he brought about in her. What if those changes disappeared now that he was out of her life? Who would keep her accountable? He was the only one who saw the differences.

Gavin nervously approached their table. He kept shooting glances over his shoulder like he didn't want anyone to see him. "Keeley, can we talk? Privately?"

"If this is about Talon, I don't have anything to say. I still can't believe you're related."

"Please?" he begged. "It'll only take a minute or two."

Reluctantly, she agreed. What did she have to lose? She followed him to an empty classroom and sat down in one of the seats.

Gavin clasped his hands together, almost like he was getting ready to make a speech. "I know you don't want to hear about JT, but I think you should know he really cares about you."

"That's not the issue." She knew his feelings for her were real. That's what made it so hard.

"He still carries around a lot of guilt for what he did to Claire. He doesn't talk about it, but he's different now."

That caught her attention. "What do you mean?"

"When he found out about Claire and Zach, he was angry, even volatile, but after he sent those photos ..." His face tightened as if in pain. "He became resigned, as if being an asshole was his lot in life. There's a huge difference between the guy who moved here and the guy he is now. When you guys started dating, it was like having the old Talon back. Don't judge him based off one mistake that's in the past."

Keeley knew what it was like to try to change. But still ... "You can't just sweep things under the rug and pretend they're not there. He did what he did. And it's not just that. The fact that he sent those pictures in the first place makes me worried. I know he was upset but it doesn't make it okay."

"Haven't you ever been so angry you did things you didn't mean?" Gavin argued, his eyes flashing.

"But I didn't act upon it. There's a huge difference." She couldn't keep arguing about this with him. She did enough of that by herself. "Gavin, I appreciate what you're trying to do, but it's over."

"But he tried to fix it! He tried to get people to stop sending them around. Doesn't that count for anything?"

It did count; but, it didn't take away what he did, either. Those pictures were still out there. That girl's life was still ruined.

"Just think about what I said, okay?" Gavin was almost out the door when he stopped. Turning around, he gave a sheepish expression. "One last question — are you going to tell Zach about me? Being related to Talon and helping him with the prank?"

That was a good question. One she didn't have an answer for. She realized how much hell Gavin would be put through if the football team found out, but at the same time, she made that promise with Zach. No more secrets. She weighed her options. At the end of the day, her relationship with Zach was more important. "I'm going to have to tell him. I'm sorry, Gavin."

His shoulders slumped. "I figured. Oh well."

When Keeley sat back down at the table, Nicky asked, "What did he want?"

"Trying to get me back together with Talon."

"I hope you told him no."

"Of course." But some of Gavin's words had struck a chord with her. At what point does a person get forgiven? Can they be forgiven? And even if she was to forgive Talon, how could she ever trust him again?

Chapter 24

iGet a Surprise

...

It was the night of Homecoming. Keeley was on the couch eating ice cream when the doorbell rang. It was probably Zach and his hands were too full to open the door. He'd gone to pick up their food at the Chinese restaurant around the block. When he found out she was staying home by herself, he'd canceled his date and insisted on spending the night with her. She quickly paused the show to answer the door.

"Claire," she whispered, recognizing the girl in Zach's picture. Same delicate features and silky straight hair.

Surprise registered on her face. "You know who I am."

"I've heard about you."

Claire flinched, and Keeley would have missed it if she hadn't been watching closely. "I see," she murmured. And Keeley had a sense she did see. She saw the whole complicated picture. A few uncomfortable moments passed before she asked, "Can I come in?"

Keeley's hand tightened around the doorknob. "Zach's not here."

There was nothing small about the flinch this time. Claire's whole body reared back as if struck by a two-by-four. "I know. I saw him leave."

That must mean she's here to talk to me, Keeley thought. She studied Claire. There was no doubt she was pretty, but she wasn't gorgeous like so many of the girls her brother dated. However, there was something about her that made a person stop and stare. Keeley couldn't put her finger on it, but whatever it was, it radiated from within.

Keeley stepped aside. "Can I get you anything? Water? Soda? Juice?" she asked as she ushered her to the living room. Tucker followed hot on their heels.

Claire ran a hand over her sweater, smoothing out invisible wrinkles. "No, thank you. I had some water on the drive over."

It struck Keeley as funny that they were acting like a couple of adults. Clearly, they were both nervous and trying to cover it up with good manners. She sat down on the couch and Claire picked the chair across the way. She smoothed her sweater again as her eyes darted around the room. Keeley patiently sat there, determined to let Claire speak first and set the tone of the conversation. After all, she was the one who had shown up unexpectedly. It was her show.

"You know, I've always wondered what the inside of your house looked like," Claire finally said.

"Zach never brought you here?"

A wistful look entered her eyes. "He always wanted to meet somewhere else. I asked one time if we could come here so I could meet you, and he told me he wasn't ready to share me yet."

"That doesn't surprise me," Keeley replied, rubbing her sweaty hands against the back of her shirt. "He's never been good about sharing his things."

"I see," Claire said softly.

When she didn't go on, Keeley asked, "So you wanted to meet me when you guys were …" What exactly did she call what they did? Dating? Two-timing?

Claire's eyes, the shade of dark honey, flashed. "He was always talking about you. I wanted to be friends." She looked away, her body tense. "But I guess there's no chance of that happening now."

This conversation was every bit as awkward as Keeley thought it would be. She fiddled with the tassels of a pillow, wondering what to say. *Conscious choice*, she told herself. *Be bold*. "Claire, why did you come here? Is this about Zach? Talon? Or both?"

She didn't answer for a long time. Keeley wondered if she was going to talk at all, but then she jetted out a breath and swallowed. "I'm sure you know what happened between your brother, JT and I. It's not exactly a big secret around here."

The pain carved in Claire's face called out to Keeley. "It's not as widespread as you think," she assured her. "I didn't even know what happened until recently."

Claire's look of gratitude humbled her. Clearly, this girl had been through a lot. It showed not only in her expression, but also in the way she dressed. She wore an oversized sweater, baggy jeans and running shoes. The only skin showing was on her hands, neck and face. Like she didn't want anyone to see her.

"I've tried hard to forget what happened and move on with my life." Claire's head tilted down so she could stare at the floor. "But something always crops back up and makes its way to the surface. It can be a photo or rumors or running into someone from here." Her hand trembled as she reached up and brushed the bangs out of her eyes.

It was clear she'd been through a lot. "I'm so sorry," Keeley whispered. "I can't imagine what you've been through."

Tucker padded over to Claire and put his head on her lap. Claire's face softened and she reached down to pet him. "I used to lie awake at night thinking of what I would do if I ever came face-to-face with JT again. I thought of yelling at him, calling him all sorts of names, punching him in the face and even stealing his stash of Peeps." She gave Tucker one last scratch behind the ears before straightening. "But the truth is when he came to my house two days ago, I didn't do any of that."

Keeley's stomach clenched. "You saw him?"

"I didn't want to at first. But I realized I had to if I was ever going to move on for real."

Why would Talon visit Claire? And why would she come here after that? Keeley's mind filled with questions.

"We talked. About me, about him, about your brother." She lifted her gaze. "And about you. I got a lot off my chest. And I realized all those nights I lay awake, I wasn't looking for a chance to yell at him, but a chance to move on. I was stuck in this loop of hating him and myself, and it never ended. And it wasn't until I saw him that I realized in order to move on, I needed to forgive." Her eyes glowed with determination. "And I have. I forgive JT."

Good for Claire, and good for Talon, but Keeley was still confused. "How do I fit into all of this?"

"JT told me about how he kept you in the dark for most of your relationship."

"Try all," Keeley corrected.

"Out of the four hours we talked, two of them were about you. I won't go into specifics, but he told me how you two met, how he fell for you, your time at Barnett and even about your first date. A little rude considering I'm his ex-girlfriend" — she laughed a little — "but I didn't mind that much. Especially when I heard about all the times you put him in his place."

Keeley's lips twitched. She'd had such a great time messing with him.

"The reason why I came here today was to tell you that JT has changed. He's not the same guy I knew three years ago."

Her smile faded. "Did he ask you to come here and say this to me?"

"He doesn't know I'm here. I've made peace with JT. He apologized for what he did and he really is sorry. I believe him."

Claire leaned forward in her chair, her face earnest. "I get why you broke up with him. I would have done the same thing, too, but now that you know the worst about him and all the cards are on the table, can't you forgive him?"

"But what he did to you and how he used me —"

"I know," Claire said quietly. Briefly, she glanced at a picture of Zach that was hanging on the wall. "I know all about boys who use you, but JT genuinely cares for you."

"But he cared about you, too, and look what happened."

"He made a mistake — a stupid, idiotic, rage-induced mistake. I'm not saying it was okay, but I think he's learned from it." She placed a hand over her heart. "I'm telling you as a girl, as someone who's made plenty of mistakes myself, that JT's changed."

Keeley's mind was spinning. "I have to be honest. You're not what I expected at all."

Claire threw her head back and laughed. "I'll take that as a compliment."

"Can I ask you a personal question?" Keeley prayed she wouldn't get too offended.

Her face sobered. "You can ask."

"Why didn't you break up with Talon when you started having feelings for my brother?" She'd wondered that for a long time now.

Claire looked out the window. The ends of her mouth turned slightly down. "You know, I ask myself that, too. I could have avoided a lot of pain if I had." Her hands clenched in her lap. "I told myself I was doing JT a favor by not breaking up with him. He was really upset about moving and his grandpa's death. I convinced myself breaking up would only hurt him more. But the truth is I stayed because I was insecure."

"What do you mean?" Keeley asked.

"I was never the girl that guys chased after, especially back then. In middle school, I had these horrible braces and glasses ..." She shuddered. "It was awful. But freshman year, I got contacts and my braces came off. Suddenly, I was the one guys looked at, and not just any guy, but JT. He blew everyone else out of the water."

Keeley's teeth clenched. Hearing about the two of them together was harder than she thought. But she knew what Claire was saying. How special it feels to be liked by Talon.

"When he asked me to be his girlfriend, I couldn't believe it. All these girls around him, and he chose me. Everything was fine at first but then the girls started getting more aggressive. They would do all sorts of things to try and attract him."

Keeley wouldn't know. They'd spent most of their relationship hiding so Zach wouldn't find out.

"I felt I needed to do something extreme to keep his interest so I sent those photos." Claire sighed. "Worst mistake of my life. After I sent them, I felt ... dirty. Everyone thinks it will bring you closer together, but it did the opposite. I pulled away and that's when I met your brother. He was my chance at a fresh start. A way to get away from JT and those awful photos. But being with Zach while staying with JT was selfish."

Claire ran a hand through her hair, pulling it out from behind her ear and letting it fall around her face. "As much as JT hurt me, I hurt him, too. That's why I'm here. Trying to make amends for cheating on him."

Keeley took a deep breath. She didn't know if what Claire said changed anything, but she appreciated hearing this. It gave her a lot to think about.

Claire put her hands on her knees and stood up. "I should get going. Thanks for hearing me out."

As Keeley walked her to the door, Claire held out a white envelope with a large bulge in the corner. "Oh, and before I forget, can you give your brother this?"

Keeley took the envelope but didn't peek inside. She knew it was Zach's class ring. "Why are you giving it back now?" Claire had kept it for almost three years.

"I think I held on to it so I wouldn't forget the bad choices I made. But forgiving JT made me realize I have to forgive myself, too." Claire paused, her hand lingering on the door frame. "Good luck, Keeley."

Keeley went back to the couch and sank down, trying to absorb everything Claire told her. Had Talon changed? Could she truly trust him now? After all, Claire, the girl he hurt the most, forgave him. Did that mean she could as well? She was in the same spot when Zach finally returned.

"I'm back," Zach yelled, tossing his keys on the dining room table. He put the bags of Chinese food on the coffee table in front of Keeley. "You won't believe how long the line was." He took out the containers and opened them. "Can you get the plates, Keels?"

She clutched the envelope in her hand. She almost wished Claire had kept his ring. This was going to bring up a lot of memories for him. Ones she wasn't sure he was ready for.

"Keels?"

Keeley's leg started to bounce as she fingered the white envelope. "Zach, uh ... I — Well ... here." She shoved the envelope into his lap.

"What is it?" he asked, holding it up in the air.

"Something for you." When he narrowed his eyes, she said, "Just open it."

"You're acting weird," he muttered, but did as she directed. His face went white when he saw what was inside. His piercing eyes turned to her, holding her in her place. "How did you get this?" he asked.

"Claire stopped by while you were out."

"She was here? What did she say?" The eagerness on his face nearly broke her heart.

Keeley hesitated, unsure of what to tell him. "She wanted to talk about Talon and she wanted me to give you the envelope."

Understanding dawned on his face. "She's moving on," he said, his eyes blinking rapidly. "This is her telling me goodbye."

Keeley stood and wrapped her arms around her twin. She rubbed his back as his breathing turned ragged, each exhale heavy with emotion. "Maybe this is a good thing. Now you can move on, too."

"I can't get her out of my head. Haven't you ever liked someone so much that when you make them smile or laugh, you feel like you're the king of the world? That's how I feel about Claire. That feeling doesn't just go away. It grabs hold and sticks with you."

"Yeah," replied Keeley sadly. "I know exactly what you mean."

Chapter 25

iTake a Leap

• • •

Keeley's fingers tapped the table as she stared at the school library door waiting for Gavin. How long did it take to get here? She'd been patiently waiting for thirty minutes and the morning bell was about to ring. They were running out of time.

"Are you sure you want to do this?" Nicky asked.

"Positive," she stated. She knew Nicky didn't agree, but she was through caring what other people thought. She believed what Claire said. Talon had changed and so had she. Keeley still didn't know what she wanted to do after high school, but she knew what she wanted right now. A lot more Talon in her life.

Keeley shook her head and went back to staring at the door. She was getting nervous. Hell, who was she kidding? She was way past nervous and heading straight toward worried. Her whole plan hinged on this. What if he didn't follow through? The library door opened and Gavin walked in.

"Do you have his phone?" Keeley asked.

Gavin pushed his hood down and set his backpack on the floor. He pursed his lips and stared at her for a couple beats before saying, "I want to go on the record and say I don't like this. Not one bit."

"Aren't you the one who said I needed to make up with him?" She remembered when Talon told her about his girl cousin who played football. Keeley had said she didn't think she could make a big statement like that, but he pointed out it just had to be big to her. Well, this was her big statement. She was letting all her emotions out. She just hoped he felt the same.

"Yes, but I thought you'd just talk to him. Not this." He handed her the phone. It seemed a lifetime ago when she last had it. Back when Talon was just Talon, a mysterious voice on the other end.

"How'd you get it?" she asked.

"I pretended to forget a book at his house and ran over there this morning. He almost caught me going through his stuff, but luckily his mom called us downstairs. I still don't understand how this is supposed to get you two back together," Gavin said.

"You'll see." Before she gave Gavin her phone last night, she'd made a few changes to her settings. When Talon used it, he would constantly be reminded of her. It could be pictures of them on her background, or alarms randomly going off with inside jokes and heartfelt messages, or ringtones that held special meanings. Hopefully her phone showed Talon what he was missing.

216

Nicky eyed her. "Do you want to look through his texts? See if he has any other secrets?"

"He told me he has nothing to hide and I believe him."

"You sure?"

"Absolutely."

Keeley sighed. Talon hadn't texted her yet and she was getting worried. It was already the last class of the day. She'd set twenty-five alarms to go off. There was no way he could turn them off without the password, which he didn't have. She'd expected a voice mail or *something* by now. Had she waited too long? Was there no hope of getting him back?

No. She couldn't believe it. Not after he reads the messages she posted with those alarms. Keeley had poured her heart out into those messages, spending hours last night writing and rewriting till each one was perfect. She had never been so honest in her life.

A wad of paper hit her forehead. "What?" she mouthed to Nicky. She quickly glanced at Mrs. Miller, but she was writing on the whiteboard.

"It flashed," Nicky mouthed back, pointing to Keeley's lap. Keeley was nervous as she discreetly looked at the phone. Was it finally him?

Talon: What the hell I like you? Why do I have your Keeley's amazing?

Damn it! What did you do to my Keeley's amazing?

She wanted to laugh, but she pressed her lips together, holding it in. It seemed her prank was working. She'd gone into her phone settings and changed a few keywords so that every time he typed a certain word or phrase, the phone would autocorrect to whatever she'd programmed. Her name automatically changed to "I like you" and "phone" changed to "Keeley's amazing."

Aww thank you! And no need to gush …
I already know how amazing I am. 😊

No! This is not happening. I want
my Keeley's amazing back.

Well, if you insist …

I like you! This is not funny.
Change. This. Immediately.

I know! Feelings and emotions aren't funny
at all. They need to be taken very seriously,
which is why I take your confession to heart.

You are the most beautiful girl I've ever met!

Keeley struggled to keep quiet. She knew he would use the word "impossible."

> Your words are making me blush.

> Those are YOUR words. Not mine.

> I don't know what you're talking about. All I know is that the guy I like keeps complimenting me.

> I like you …

> I like you too …

Keeley dropped the phone in her lap when Mrs. Miller passed by. She was handing back the revised admission essays they wrote.

At the very top of Keeley's paper was a big fat A+. In the margin, Mrs. Miller had scribbled, "Great job connecting the two." She'd written that by making a conscious decision to embrace her fear, she allowed herself to move on.

"What'd you get?" Zach asked, turning around. She proudly showed him the paper. He whistled, looking impressed. "I only got an A–."

"I scored higher than you?" She was shocked. That had never happened before. She couldn't wait to show her parents. Hell, she might even tack it on the fridge.

As Mrs. Miller continued to pass out papers, Keeley peeked at the phone again.

> Why did you do this? You broke up with me, remember?

I heard you went to see Claire. I thought it was very brave to own up to your mistakes.

I didn't do it for you.

That's what makes it meaningful.

What are you trying to say here?

I think we have something worth fighting for.

How do I know you're not going to change your mind and break up with me again?

She thought about the moments on the beach when she learned the truth about Talon and Claire.

You're scared. Afraid to trust. I get that.

You don't.

I do. I broke up with you for the same reason and do you remember what you asked me? You asked me to trust you. I'm asking you to do the same thing.

Why should I give you what you refused to give me?

Well, crap. That was a really good question. But there were never any guarantees ... for anything. That didn't mean you shouldn't try.

> We're at the edge of a cliff, Talon. It's either take a leap and try to reach the other side or fall apart and lose what we have.

> Haven't you heard the higher you go, the harder you fall?

> It's a risk I'm willing to take. I don't know what else to do or say that will convince you but I'm all in, Talon.

> Did you really mean this?

There was a picture attached to his text. It was a screenshot of one of her messages. A poem. The first one she had ever attempted to write. Maybe it wasn't great, but it summed up everything she was feeling.

> When I say three little words, I become giddy inside.
> It's such an amazing feeling I cannot hide.
> When I say three little words, a smile comes to my face.
> It's an immediate reaction no matter the place.
> When I say three little words, my problems start to fade away.
> These three little words brighten my day.
> When I say three little words, I want you to be about,
> Because those three little words you should never doubt.

Her adrenaline spiked. She felt vulnerable. Exposed.

Every word.

And this?

Another screenshot.

> There are a lot of qualities I admire in a person, but one of the biggest is the ability to say you're sorry. I'm not talking about the quick apologies people say when they accidentally bump into someone, but the deep, heartfelt apologies that strip you of your ego and humble you before a person you've wronged.
>
> I know you feel guilty for what happened. I know you carry around shame. But despite what you think, you deserve forgiveness. You've paid your dues. Let yourself be happy, and if you can't, at least allow me to be by your side so I can show you.

Yes.

And you're positive this is what you want? You and me? No take-backs or second-guessing?

100% positive. Will you jump with me?

"What's going on?" Nicky whispered on the way out of class. Concern was etched in every word. "What did he say?"

"I'm just waiting." Keeley gripped the phone. Waiting was going to kill her.

"Waiting for what?" asked Nicky.

As long as you're with me.

Keeley's face broke out in a huge grin.

"Keeley?" Nicky pressed. "Waiting for what?"

"To take a leap."

Chapter 26

iAm Caught

•••

Keeley took one look in the mirror and ripped out the bobby pins holding her brown locks back. Twenty minutes she'd been standing in the bathroom, curling and fidgeting with her hair, and what did she have to show for it? Absolutely nothing. If anything, her hair looked worse. Normally, she would put it in a bun and call it a day, but today wasn't any day. In exactly thirty minutes, she would be meeting with Talon for the first time since sending those texts.

Her skin tingled with equal parts excitement and nerves. The meeting felt monumental, even bigger than their first date. All the secrets, all the dirty laundry were out in the open. There were no more excuses for running away. This was it. They could finally build a relationship on an even playing field. Nothing was holding them back.

Now if only I could tame this beast, she thought to herself. She grabbed a hairbrush and started untangling the knots.

Ten minutes later, she headed downstairs with a sore scalp and what felt like ten pounds of hairspray. When she went into the living room to get her purse, she passed by her brother, who was parked in front of the TV, lying on the couch in the same position she'd seen him in since breakfast.

"You going somewhere?" he asked idly, one hand behind his head, the other on a remote, flipping through channels.

"The pier."

"How about I drive you?" He dropped the remote and sat up. "I need to get out of the house."

"I'm going to the boardwalk. You're staying here." Away from Talon.

His eyes narrowed as he studied her face. Something must have tipped him off because seconds later he groaned. "This again? I thought he was over and done with."

"I know you don't like him and that's fine." She'd accepted the fact they would never get along. "But your feelings do not factor into my relationship with him, just as his feelings do not factor into ours."

"It matters," he argued. "How can it not?"

She didn't want to bring up a painful topic, but he left her no choice. "What if Claire wanted to get back together and I told you I didn't like her?"

His nose wrinkled. "You have no reason not to like her. She's never done anything to you."

"But if I didn't?" she pushed. "What then? Would you tell her no? Walk away?"

He pressed his lips together.

"See? It's not that easy. I'm going after what I want. I love you, but I have to do what makes me happy, and Talon makes me happy."

He lifted his head and looked her in the eye, a sad smile pasted on his face. "I'm going to go walk Tucker. I'll see you later."

"Wait, Zach —"

But he was already out the door with the leash in hand. So instead she grabbed her purse and went to meet Talon.

He was already waiting for her by the time she pulled into the parking lot. His posture was relaxed as he sat on a bench, quietly observing the waves, a pack of Peeps next to him. He didn't look nervous at all. Maybe she was the only one who thought this was a big deal. As she walked up to him, Keeley noticed he kept glancing down at his hands and then rolling his shoulders.

"Hey," she said hesitantly, slowing her steps as she neared.

His head jerked up at the sound of her voice and he exhaled. "You made it."

"I did." She rounded the bench and stopped, not sure what she should do. What exactly was the protocol for seeing an ex-boyfriend when you were about to get back together? Should she hug him? Not touch him at all? Offer a polite handshake? Make a joke?

He jumped out of his seat and shoved something into his pocket — her phone. Her eyes widened as she caught a glimpse of the screen. It was text messages from her. He'd been rereading their texts? He gave a sheepish smile. Suddenly the tight coil of nerves she felt eased and she knew everything was going to be okay.

"Why are you way over there?" he asked.

"Because I'm waiting for my hug."

He took two long strides toward her and scooped her up in his arms, leaving her breathless. "I thought you'd never get here," he whispered.

"I know the feeling," she whispered back, blinking away tears.

Finally, he released her and they decided to take a walk along the beach.

"So what do we do now? Start over with a clean slate?" he asked, holding her hand.

"I don't think there is such a thing as a clean slate."

Talon's nose crinkled as he pulled away from her and kicked a seashell. "What are you saying? That what I did will always count against me?"

"That's not what I meant," she told him, moving closer and linking arms. "I've forgiven you for keeping secrets from me. I just don't believe we can go on acting as if it never happened. It did happen, but the difference is that we've moved on. Or at least I hope we have." She felt a muscle in his arm jerk and her lips turned down. "Have we?"

Talon opened his mouth and just as quickly closed it.

"What?" she asked, casting him an anxious glance.

He rubbed his jaw. "I think we need to discuss something before we can fully move on."

She took a deep breath and exhaled before replying. "Okay. What do you want to discuss?"

"I know you said you trust me, but do you really? Do you believe me when I say I won't ever betray you? Because I don't want to go through this again, Keeley. I need to know that you're not going to hold this over my head every time something comes up."

She tamped down the impulse to give a quick nod. He put a lot of thought into this and she needed to do the same. "I believe that you won't lie to me again, but can I ask something first?"

"Of course."

"I need you to promise you won't make decisions for me again. I don't appreciate the way everything came out about Claire. Can you do that?"

He looked into her eyes and nodded. "I can. I'll be upfront from now on."

She took hold of that promise and held it next to her heart. "Then yes, Talon, I trust you."

"Good," he murmured, bringing them to a stop, "because otherwise this could have been a really uncomfortable conversation."

She laughed and looped her hands around his neck. "And what about you? Do you trust me not to walk away again?"

He smoothed a strand of her hair and then let his hands drop to her hips. "I trust you, baby doll. You more than proved that when you stole my phone."

"I didn't steal anything."

He tugged her till she was flush against his body. Leaning down, he whispered, "Then what do you call us having each other's phones?"

Tilting her head, she whispered back, "Great planning."

"Hmmm," he murmured, capturing her lips in a kiss that made her stomach flutter. Stretching her body upward, she closed her eyes and let herself be swept away by him.

A loud whistle pierced through the air, penetrating the fog that clouded her mind. Pulling her head away, she looked over Talon's shoulder to see a group of middle schoolers watching them.

"We have an audience."

"Who cares?" he muttered, trying to kiss her again. But she dodged his attempts.

Stepping to the side, she scolded him. "They're kids!"

He rolled his eyes. "They could learn a thing or two."

This time it was her turn to roll her eyes. She grabbed his arm and moved them farther down the beach, far away from impressionable young children.

"Uh, I think someone wants to get a hold of you," Talon said. He held up her phone. There were three missed calls and four texts. She snatched it out of his hand. They were all from Zach.

When are you coming home?

Keels? You there? Need a time.

You coming back any time soon?

Stop making googly eyes at your
boyfriend and pick up your phone!

"What's wrong?" Talon asked, rubbing his hands up and down her back. She shifted closer and he started to massage her shoulders.

"Zach," she sighed, leaning into his touch.

His fingers tightened. "What does he want?"

"Who knows," she said, frustrated with her brother. Was he really going to resort to petty behavior? "He keeps asking when I'll be coming home. Like he even cares. He just wants to ruin this moment ... and I won't let him."

She didn't bother to read the next text. Probably some type of insult about Talon. She was putting her phone away when Talon grabbed her arm.

"You should text him back," he told her.

Surprised, she angled her head back so she could look at him. "Really? You want me to respond?"

"He might be worried."

"He knows I'm with you. He's only doing this to bug us."

"Probably," he acknowledged with a nod.

"There's no probably about it."

"But," he said, stressing the word, "there could be a small chance it's something else?"

Her eyes narrowed. "Why are you being so nice about this?"

He turned her around so they were facing each other. "Because if I'm going to be with you, he's going to be in the picture. Just text him back and then we can forget about him."

> I don't know when I'll be home. Why?

Are you going to be past curfew?

She glanced over at Talon, who was a few feet away rolling up his jeans. He looked up and gave her a goofy grin, pointing to a plastic pail and shovel someone had left behind.

> I don't plan on it.

Do Mom and Dad know who you're out with?

Before she could respond, he sent her another message.

I need to know what to tell them if I'm going to cover for you.

She blinked and then reread his text.

> Cover for me? You'd do that?

Well, yeah.

He would be willing to help her spend time with Talon? His one text said it all.

> I don't think I'll be late but I'll let you know if I am.

And thanks ... it means a lot.

You've had my back plenty of times.
About time I repay the favor.

Does that mean you accept Talon as my boyfriend?

Don't get ahead of yourself. Let's just
say I'll tolerate it. For now. Have fun.

As she made her way over to Talon, who was already starting to build a sand castle — or attempting to — she wondered if her brother's new attitude extended toward girls. Hopefully, he could put aside his ways and finally find one he really liked. She wanted him to have the same happiness she felt right now.

"Everything okay?" Talon asked, plopping a handful of wet sand onto another huge blob of wet sand.

She briefly told him about her conversation with Zach. He seemed as surprised as she was, but when she suggested they might turn into friends, his surprise gave way to a fierce glower.

"It could happen!" she said, winking at his dismay.

Suddenly, he picked her up by her waist and twirled her around. "Talon," she laughed, holding on to his shoulders, "what are you doing?"

"I thought it was obvious," he said, spinning her some more before gently setting her back down. "I'm celebrating."

"That my brother gave us his approval?"

"I could care less about that. No, I'm celebrating us." He dropped his forehead onto hers and clasped her hands, drawing them up to his chest. "We made it, Keeley."

Her brow furrowed. "We could have problems ... you never know ..." Edgewood and Crosswell would always be enemies. And what about college? She would be leaving. So would he.

He pressed her hands over his heart, letting her feel the steady beat. "But we can get through whatever comes our way." His tone dared her to disagree.

A surge of affection coursed through her. She reached up on her tiptoes and kissed his cheek. "Come on," she said, tugging his hand. "Let's go finish building your sand castle."

"Sand castle?!" His cheeks colored. "That's not a sand castle."

She looked at the misshapen mound and sighed with relief. "Good, because I wasn't sure how to break it to you that it looked like something out of a horror story. What were you trying to make, anyway?"

"It's a fort!" he exploded, his eyes flashing with indignation.

"Oh! Oh ..."

"It's clearly a fort! That's the watchtower." He pointed over to a small lumpy pile with rocks stacked on top. "And see? The barracks are over here and the —" While he continued to point out all essential features of the so-called fort, she silently laughed, wondering how he ever passed an art class.

"Are you listening to me?" he asked.

"Of course," she told him, managing to put on a straight face. "The barracks. How could I not see it before? It's so obvious."

A glint entered his eyes as he took a step toward her. "You, baby doll, are trouble."

"Never," she teased, taking a step back.

He started advancing, the sun bouncing off his blond hair. "Maybe you should be put in the dungeons."

"You'll have to catch me first," she taunted, running off down the beach. She heard him call her name as he started to follow, his long legs chasing her down. Laughing, she blew him a kiss and then let the boy who owned her heart catch her once and for all.

Acknowledgments

I want to personally thank the following people without whom *Textrovert* would never have seen the light of day.

To my Wattpad readers, your enthusiasm for *The Cell Phone Swap* kept me going when I wanted to throw in the towel and stop writing. Thank you for always encouraging me. You guys are the reason I write.

To the Wattpad team — especially Ashleigh Gardner, Caitlin O'Hanlon and Aron Levitz — thank you for believing in my story. You worked hard to make my dreams possible. I couldn't have done it without you.

To my editor, Kate Egan, I will never forget one of the first comments you made: "More Peeps!" I think that's when I knew you "got" my story. Thank you for showing me the ropes and making me a better writer. Your input has been invaluable.

To Lisa Lyons, you read the first draft on Wattpad, full of errors and mistakes, and still saw something worth publishing. Thank you for taking a chance on my story.

And finally, to my parents, Kollin and Joann. Your continual support has been the anchor that holds me steady. The best part of being published is seeing the pride on your faces. Thank you for everything. And no, Dad, you can't have ten percent.

wattpad

Stories you'll love

On Wattpad, you can discover stories you can't find anywhere else or create them from scratch - just like the author of this book.

Join more than 45 million people around the world who use Wattpad every day to connect with authors and create their own stories.

Connect with Lindsey Summers
wattpad.com/DoNotMicrowave

Praise for *Just a Normal Tuesday*

"There is grief and there is grace, and this book is full
of both. A look at love, loss, and learning to live with
questions that have no answers. Kim Turrisi is an
exquisite new voice."

— Martha Brockenbrough,
   author of THE GAME OF LOVE AND DEATH

kcploft.com

Keeping the Beat

FAME. LOVE. FRIENDS. PICK ANY TWO.

MARIE POWELL
& JEFF NORTON

"You're the drummer," she said to herself. "It's your job to keep them on beat. To hold it all together."

But how the bloody hell was she supposed to do that?

KCP Loft

kcploft.com

THE MORE I TOUCH SOMEONE, THE MORE I CAN SEE AND UNDERSTAND, AND THE MORE I THINK I CAN HELP.

What if one touch could tell you everything?

ZENN DIAGRAM

WENDY BRANT

BUT THAT'S MY MISTAKE. I CAN'T HELP. YOU CAN'T "FIX" PEOPLE LIKE YOU CAN SOLVE A MATH PROBLEM.

KCP Loft

kcploft.com